SUMMER CAMP SCIENCE MYSTERIES

#5 The Missing Cuckoo Clock

A Mystery about Gravity

P9-DGI-587

by Lynda Beauregard
illustrated by Der-shing Helmer

GRAPHIC UNIVERSE™ • MINNEAPOLIS

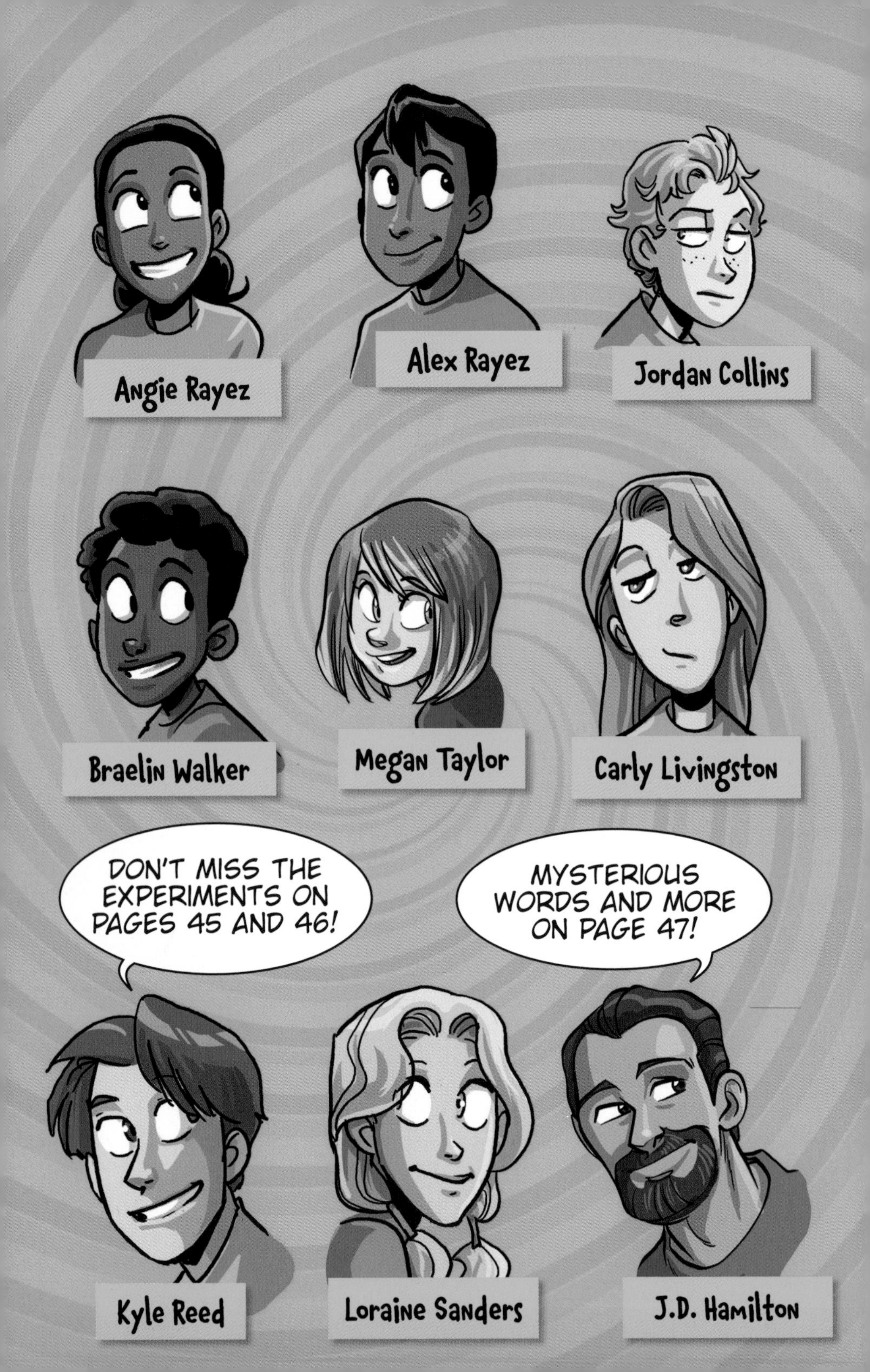
Angie Rayez
Alex Rayez
Jordan Collins
Braelin Walker
Megan Taylor
Carly Livingston
DON'T MISS THE EXPERIMENTS ON PAGES 45 AND 46!
MYSTERIOUS WORDS AND MORE ON PAGE 47!
Kyle Reed
Loraine Sanders
J.D. Hamilton

**Gravity is a force
that causes objects to pull
toward one another.**
Earth's gravity pulls on objects around Earth with
a certain amount of force, called weight. The pull of
gravity is the reason things stay on Earth's surface
instead of floating off into space.

Story by Lynda Beauregard
Art by Der-shing Helmer
Coloring by Jenn Manley Lee
Lettering by Grace Lu

Graphic Universe™
A division of Lerner Publishing Group, Inc.
241 First Avenue North
Minneapolis, MN 55401 USA

For reading levels and more information, look up this title at www.lernerbooks.com.

Main body text set in CCWildwords.
Typeface provided by Comicraft/Active Images.

Library of Congress Cataloging-in-Publication Data

Beauregard, Lynda.
      The missing cuckoo clock : a mystery about gravity / by Lynda Beauregard ; illustrated by Der-shing Helmer. — 1st American ed.
            p.   cm. — (Summer camp science mysteries ; #5)
      Summary: When the cuckoo clock from the main hall goes missing, campers, with some help from the counselors, use what they know of gravity to figure out what happened to it. Includes glossary and experiments.
      ISBN 978–1–4677–0167–9 (lib. bdg. : alk. paper)
      ISBN 978–1–4677–0980–4 (eb pdf)
      1. Graphic novels. [1. Graphic novels. 2. Camps—Fiction. 3. Gravity—Fiction.]
I. Helmer, Der-shing, ill. II. Title.
PZ7.7.B42Mis 2013
741.5'973—dc23   2012019010

Manufactured in the United States of America
2-44293-12757-5/30/2017

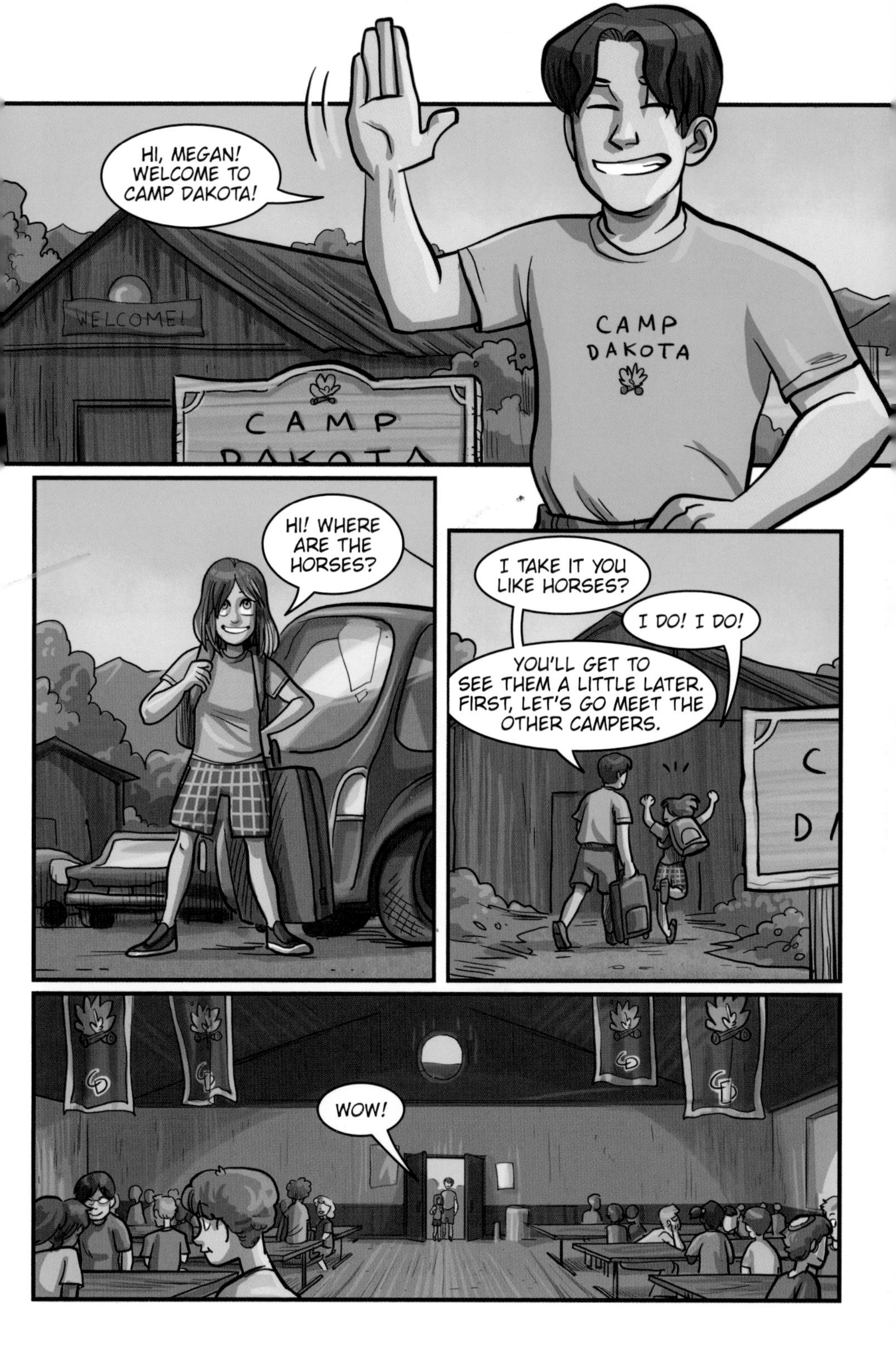
HI, MEGAN! WELCOME TO CAMP DAKOTA!
WELCOME!
CAMP DAKOTA
CAMP DAKOTA
HI! WHERE ARE THE HORSES?
I TAKE IT YOU LIKE HORSES?
I DO! I DO!
YOU'LL GET TO SEE THEM A LITTLE LATER. FIRST, LET'S GO MEET THE OTHER CAMPERS.
WOW!

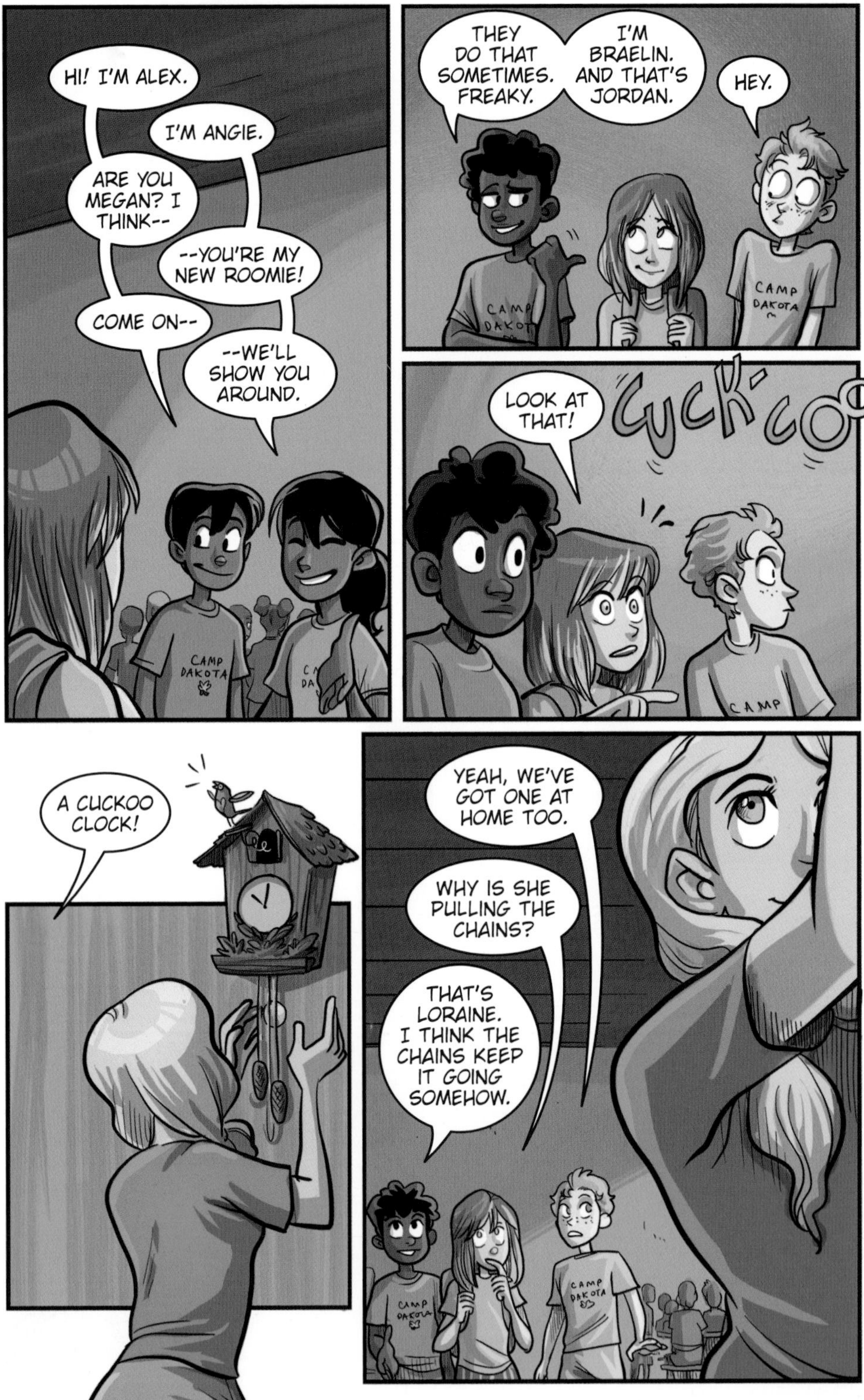
HI! I'M ALEX.
I'M ANGIE.
ARE YOU MEGAN? I THINK--
--YOU'RE MY NEW ROOMIE!
COME ON--
--WE'LL SHOW YOU AROUND.
CAMP DAKOTA
THEY DO THAT SOMETIMES. FREAKY.
I'M BRAELIN. AND THAT'S JORDAN.
HEY.
LOOK AT THAT!
CUCK-COO
A CUCKOO CLOCK!
YEAH, WE'VE GOT ONE AT HOME TOO.
WHY IS SHE PULLING THE CHAINS?
THAT'S LORAINE. I THINK THE CHAINS KEEP IT GOING SOMEHOW.

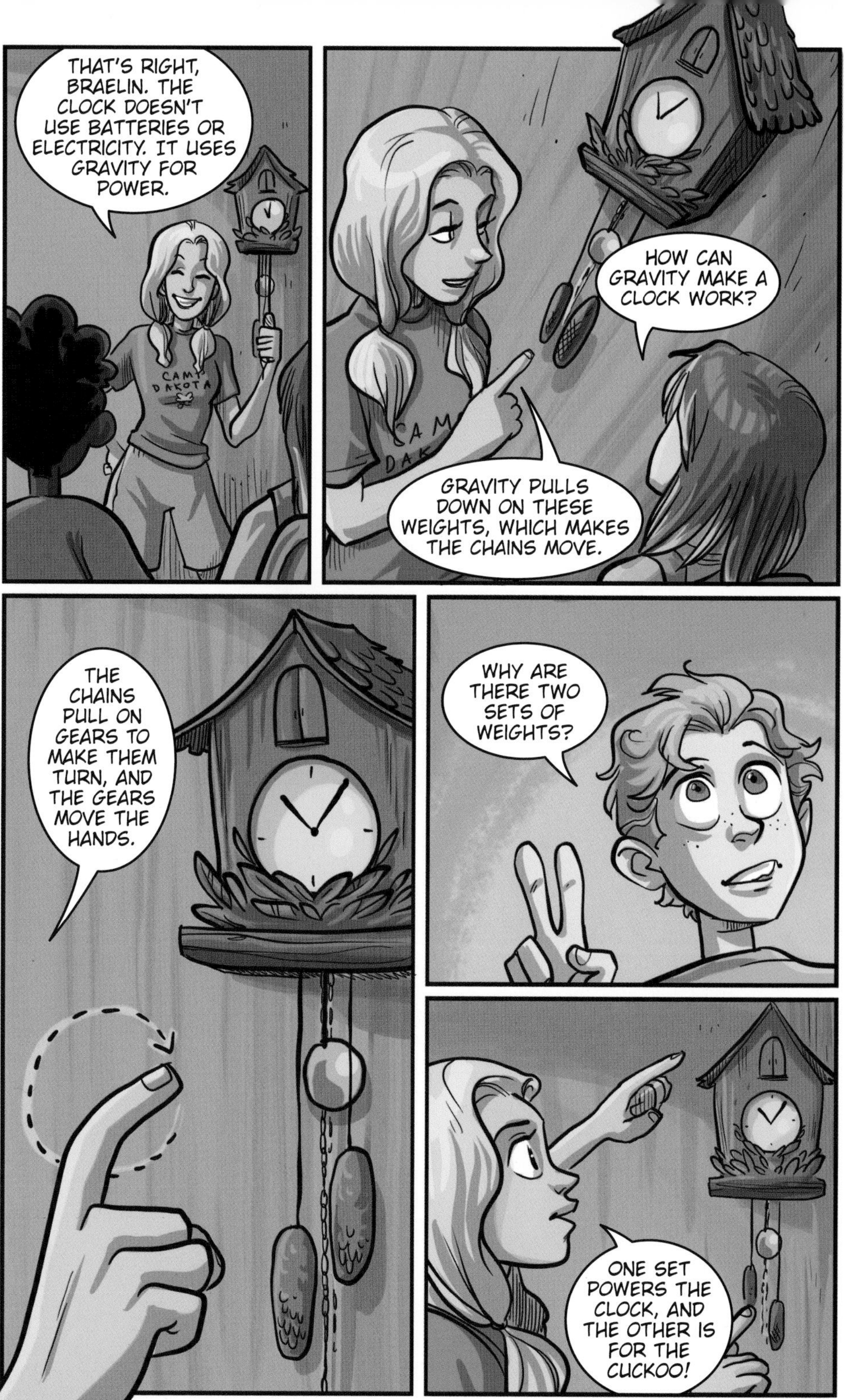
THAT'S RIGHT, BRAELIN. THE CLOCK DOESN'T USE BATTERIES OR ELECTRICITY. IT USES GRAVITY FOR POWER.
CAMP DAKOTA
HOW CAN GRAVITY MAKE A CLOCK WORK?
GRAVITY PULLS DOWN ON THESE WEIGHTS, WHICH MAKES THE CHAINS MOVE.
THE CHAINS PULL ON GEARS TO MAKE THEM TURN, AND THE GEARS MOVE THE HANDS.
WHY ARE THERE TWO SETS OF WEIGHTS?
ONE SET POWERS THE CLOCK, AND THE OTHER IS FOR THE CUCKOO!

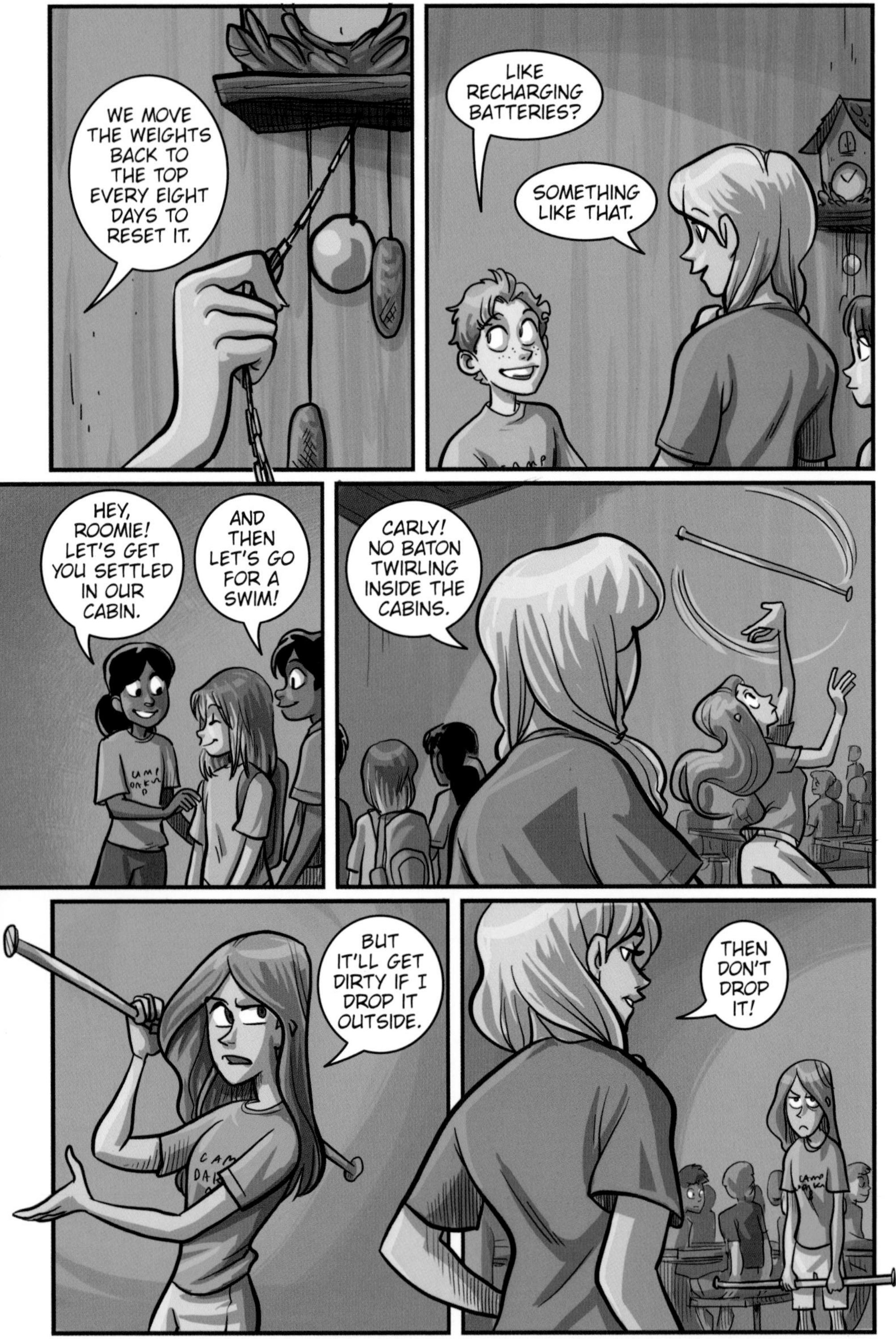
WE MOVE THE WEIGHTS BACK TO THE TOP EVERY EIGHT DAYS TO RESET IT.
LIKE RECHARGING BATTERIES?
SOMETHING LIKE THAT.
HEY, ROOMIE! LET'S GET YOU SETTLED IN OUR CABIN.
AND THEN LET'S GO FOR A SWIM!
CARLY! NO BATON TWIRLING INSIDE THE CABINS.
BUT IT'LL GET DIRTY IF I DROP IT OUTSIDE.
THEN DON'T DROP IT!

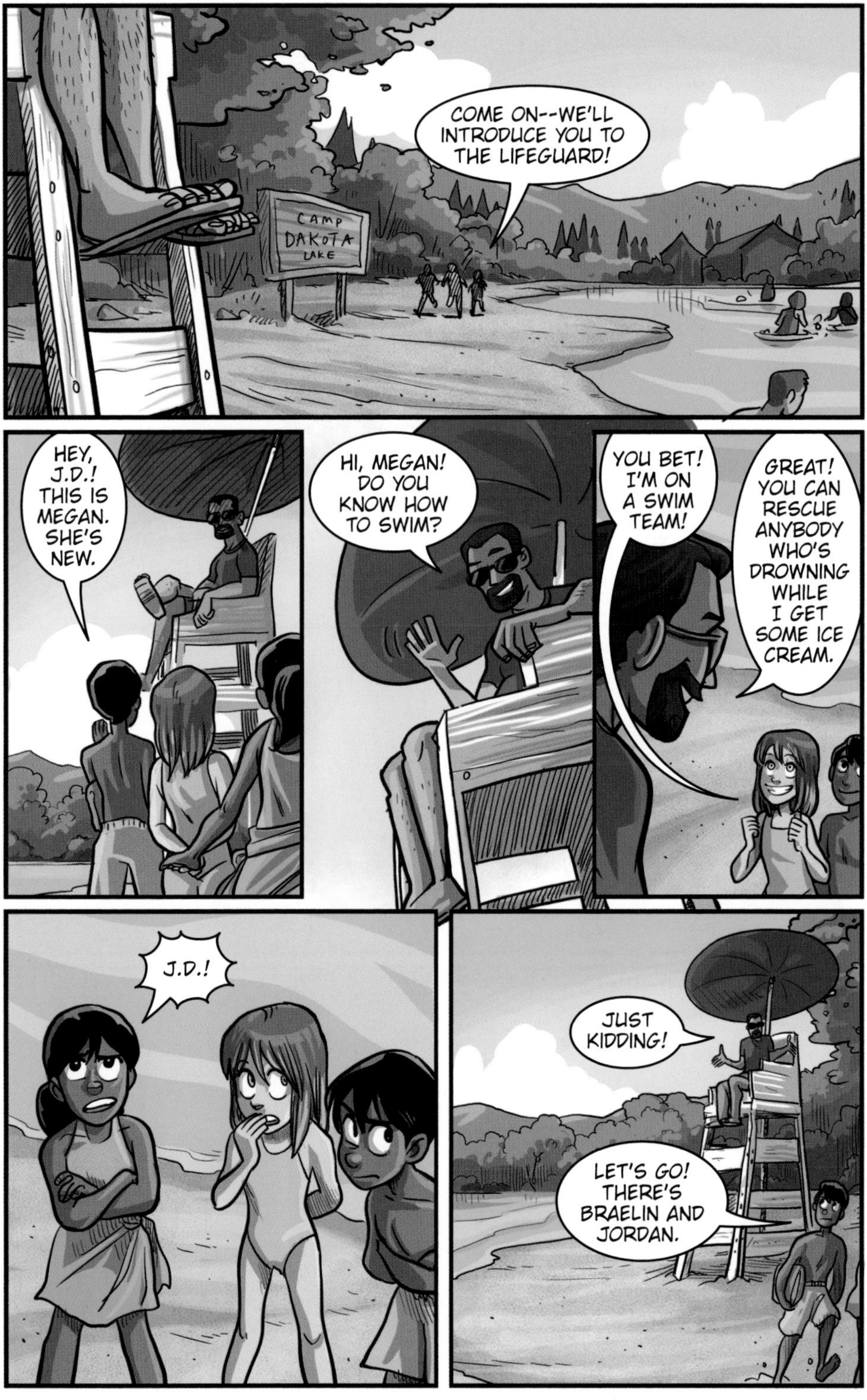
COME ON--WE'LL INTRODUCE YOU TO THE LIFEGUARD!
CAMP DAKOTA LAKE
HEY, J.D.! THIS IS MEGAN. SHE'S NEW.
HI, MEGAN! DO YOU KNOW HOW TO SWIM?
YOU BET! I'M ON A SWIM TEAM!
GREAT! YOU CAN RESCUE ANYBODY WHO'S DROWNING WHILE I GET SOME ICE CREAM.
J.D.!
JUST KIDDING!
LET'S GO! THERE'S BRAELIN AND JORDAN.

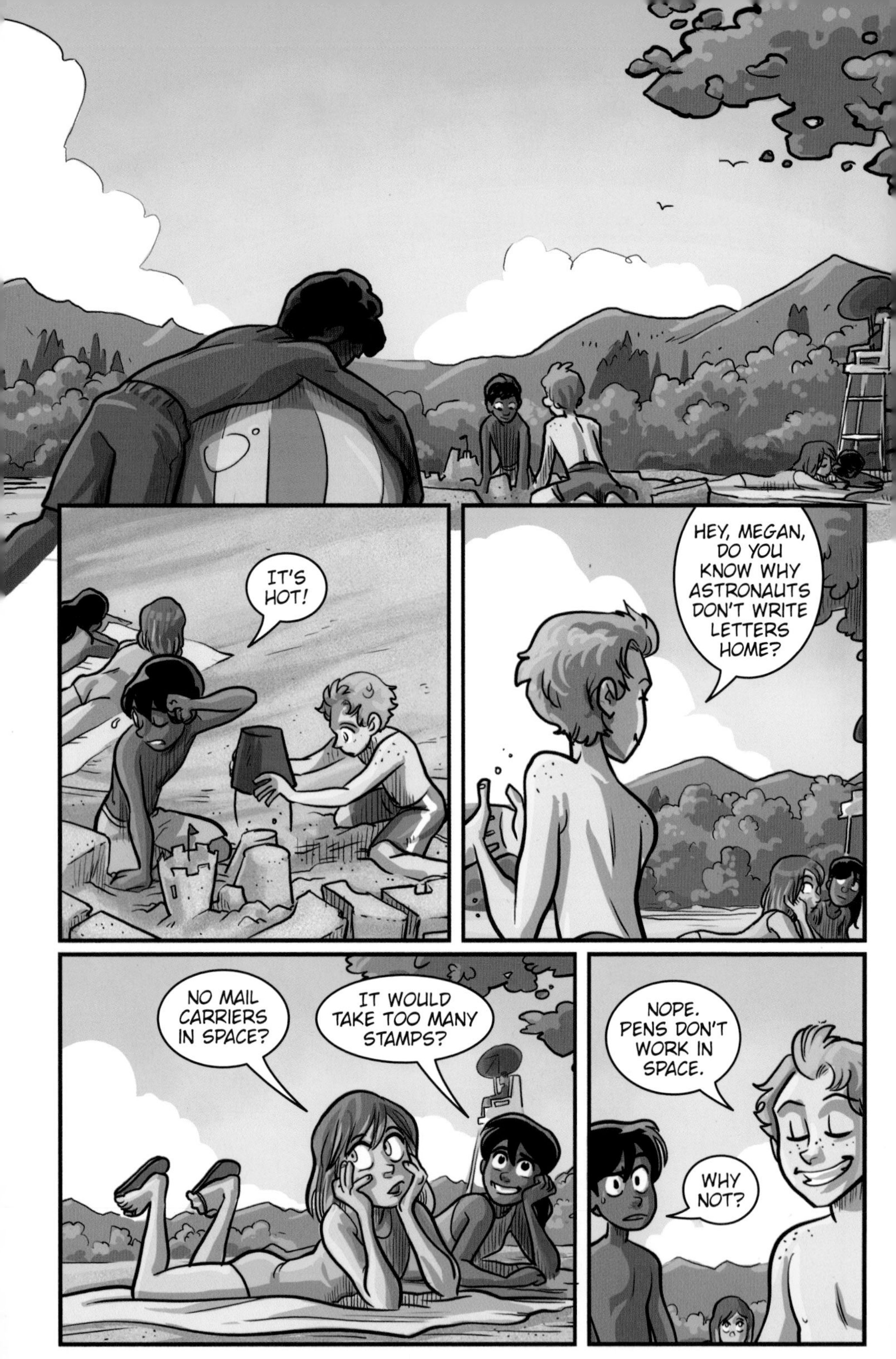
IT'S HOT!
HEY, MEGAN, DO YOU KNOW WHY ASTRONAUTS DON'T WRITE LETTERS HOME?
NO MAIL CARRIERS IN SPACE?
IT WOULD TAKE TOO MANY STAMPS?
NOPE. PENS DON'T WORK IN SPACE.
WHY NOT?

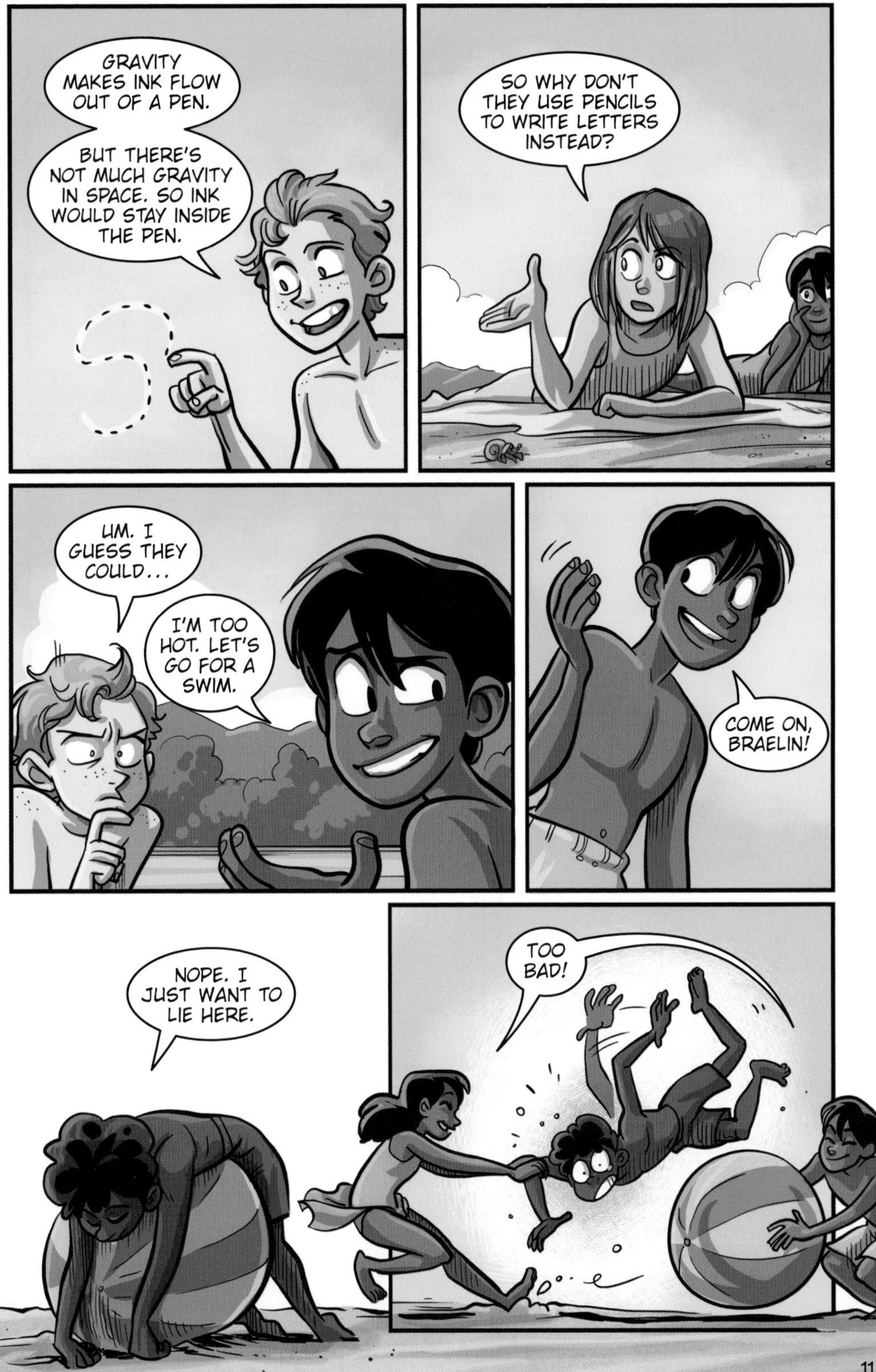
GRAVITY MAKES INK FLOW OUT OF A PEN.
BUT THERE'S NOT MUCH GRAVITY IN SPACE. SO INK WOULD STAY INSIDE THE PEN.
SO WHY DON'T THEY USE PENCILS TO WRITE LETTERS INSTEAD?
UM. I GUESS THEY COULD...
I'M TOO HOT. LET'S GO FOR A SWIM.
COME ON, BRAELIN!
NOPE. I JUST WANT TO LIE HERE.
TOO BAD!

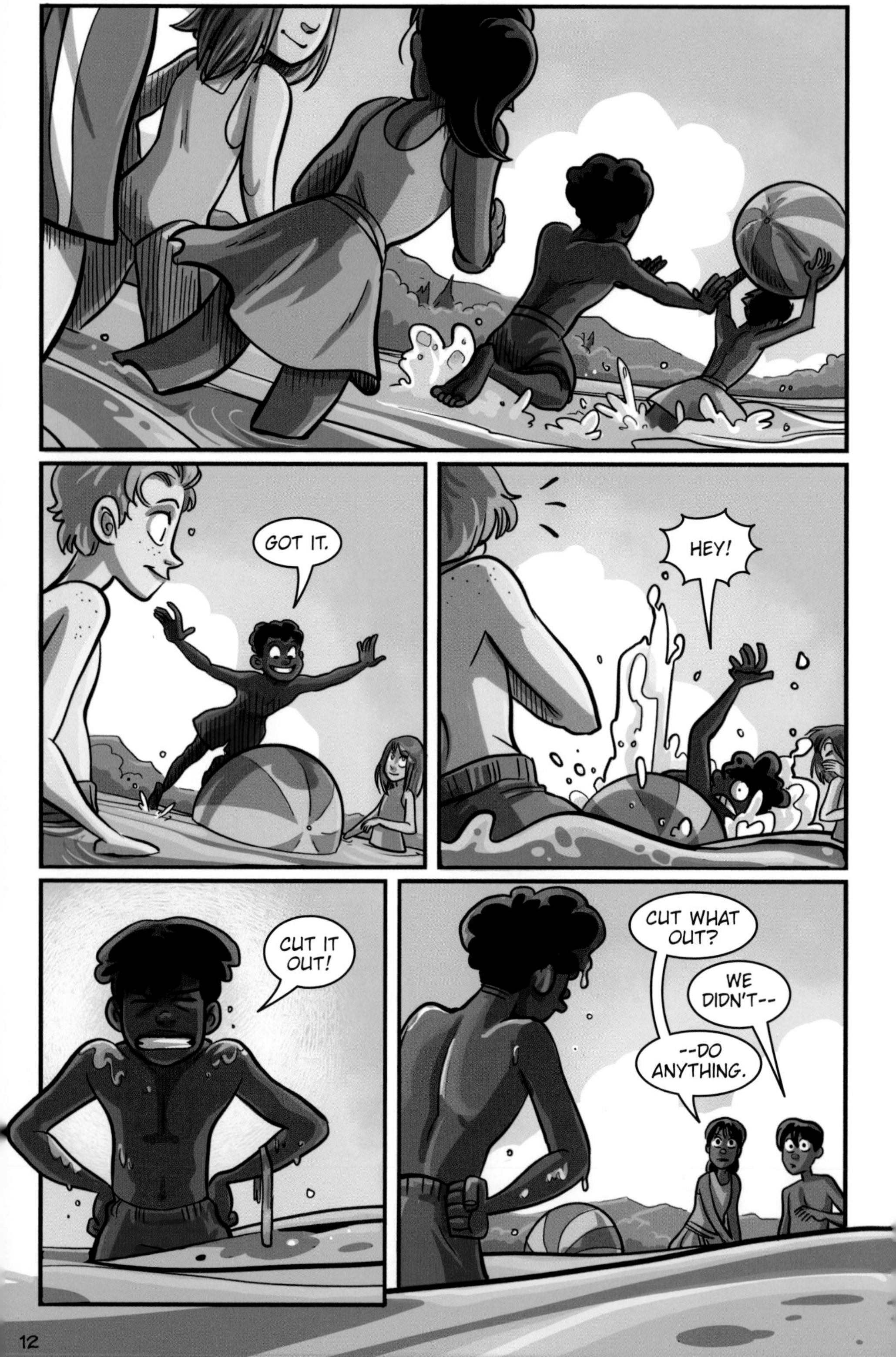
GOT IT.
HEY!
CUT IT OUT!
CUT WHAT OUT?
WE DIDN'T--
--DO ANYTHING.

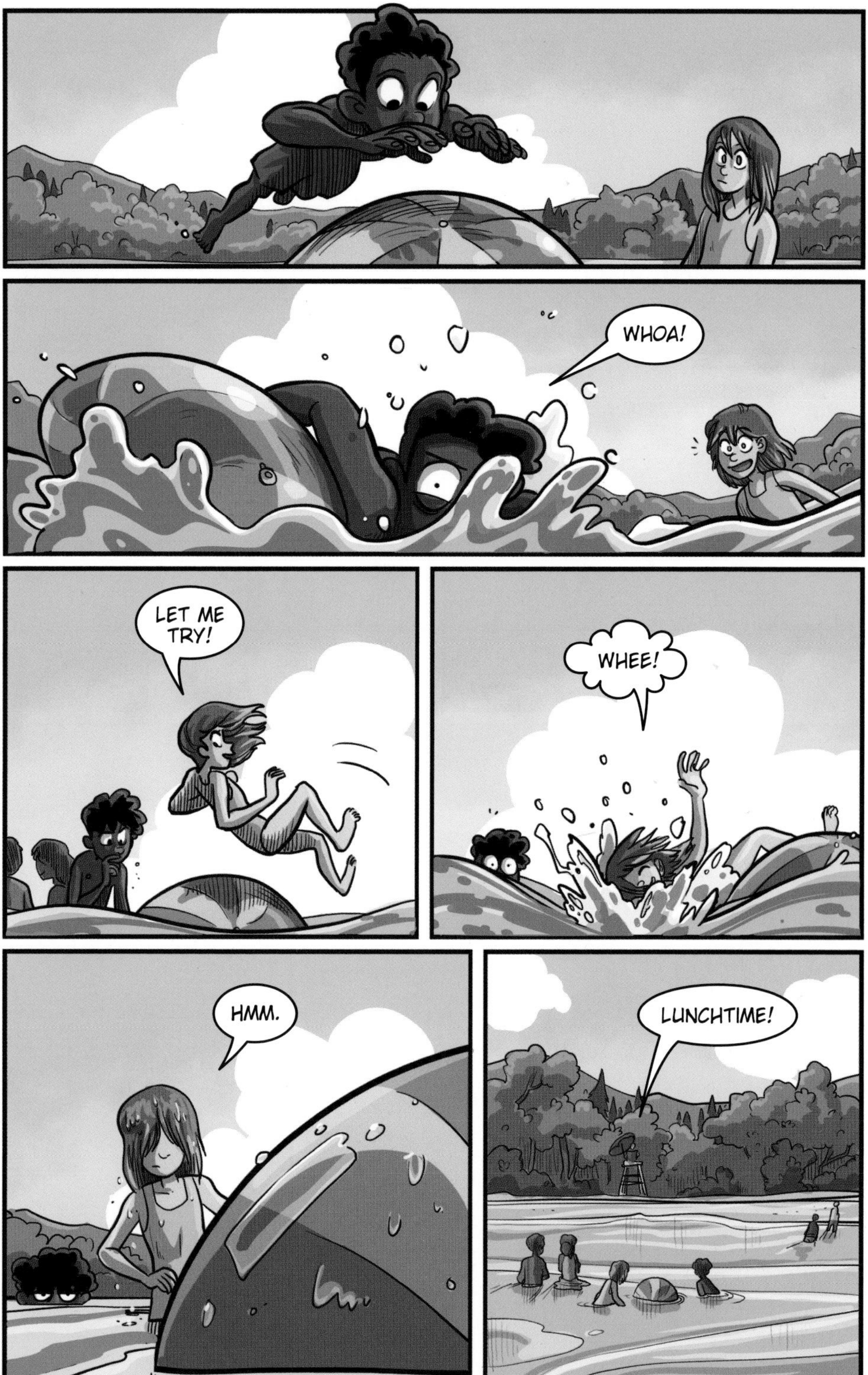
WHOA!
LET ME TRY!
WHEE!
HMM.
LUNCHTIME!

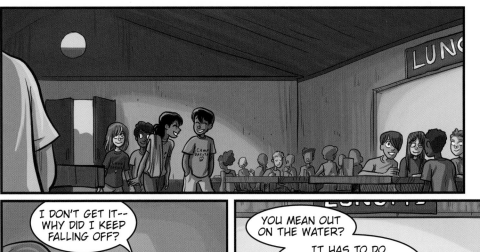

I DON'T GET IT-- WHY DID I KEEP FALLING OFF?

YOU HAD NO TROUBLE LYING ON THE BALL ON LAND.

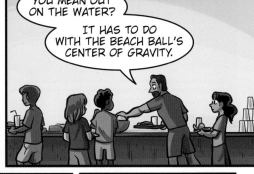

YOU MEAN OUT ON THE WATER?

IT HAS TO DO WITH THE BEACH BALL'S CENTER OF GRAVITY.

HUH?

GRAB THAT ORANGE AND I'LL SHOW YOU.

The center of gravity is the average location of an object's weight. In other words, the object's weight is evenly spread out around this spot. When an object's center of gravity is over its base, it is balanced.

OK, HERE'S OUR LAKE. PUT THE ORANGE IN IT--THAT WILL BE THE BALL.

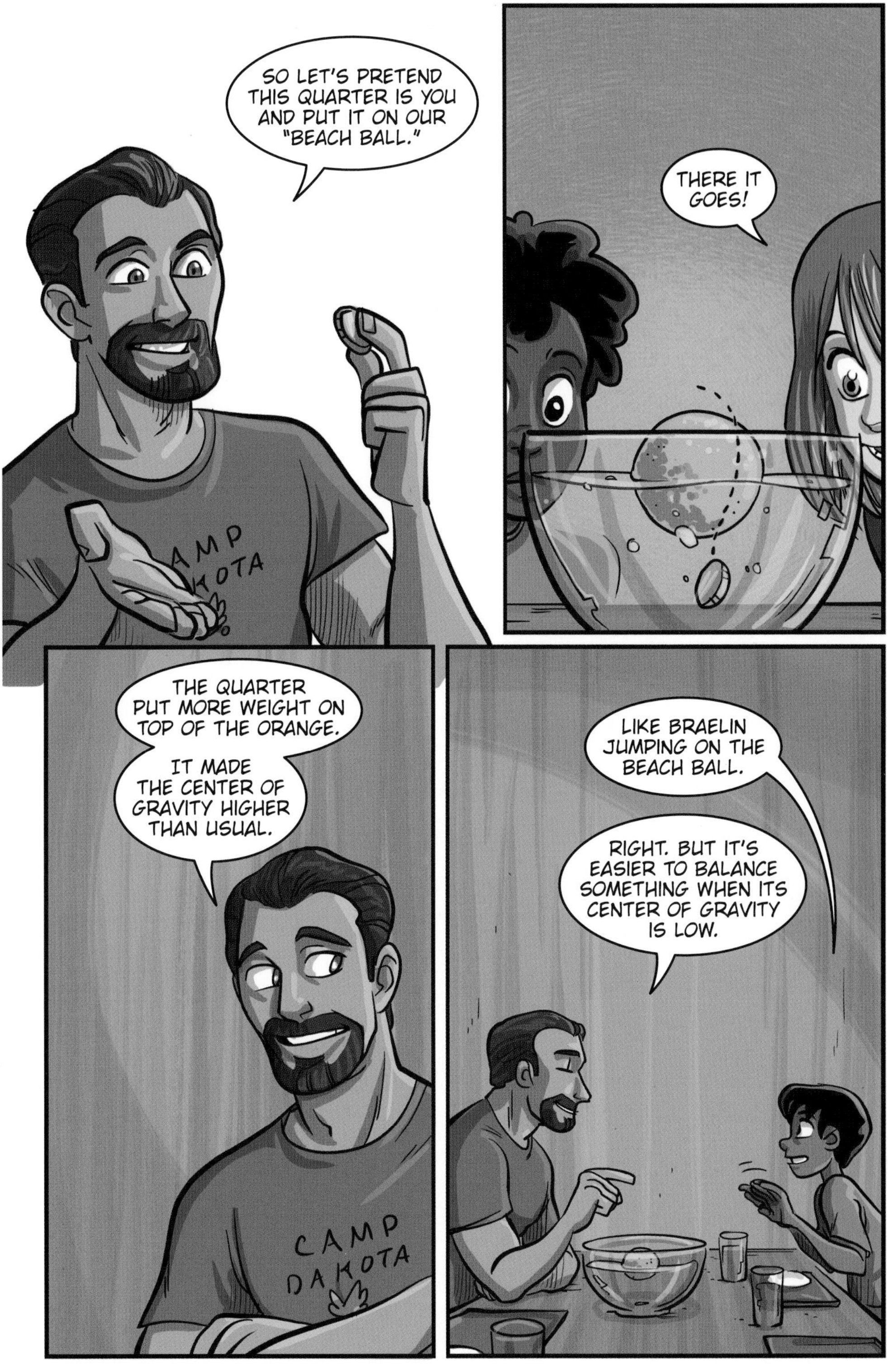
SO LET'S PRETEND THIS QUARTER IS YOU AND PUT IT ON OUR "BEACH BALL."
CAMP DAKOTA
THERE IT GOES!
THE QUARTER PUT MORE WEIGHT ON TOP OF THE ORANGE.
IT MADE THE CENTER OF GRAVITY HIGHER THAN USUAL.
CAMP DAKOTA
LIKE BRAELIN JUMPING ON THE BEACH BALL.
RIGHT. BUT IT'S EASIER TO BALANCE SOMETHING WHEN ITS CENTER OF GRAVITY IS LOW.

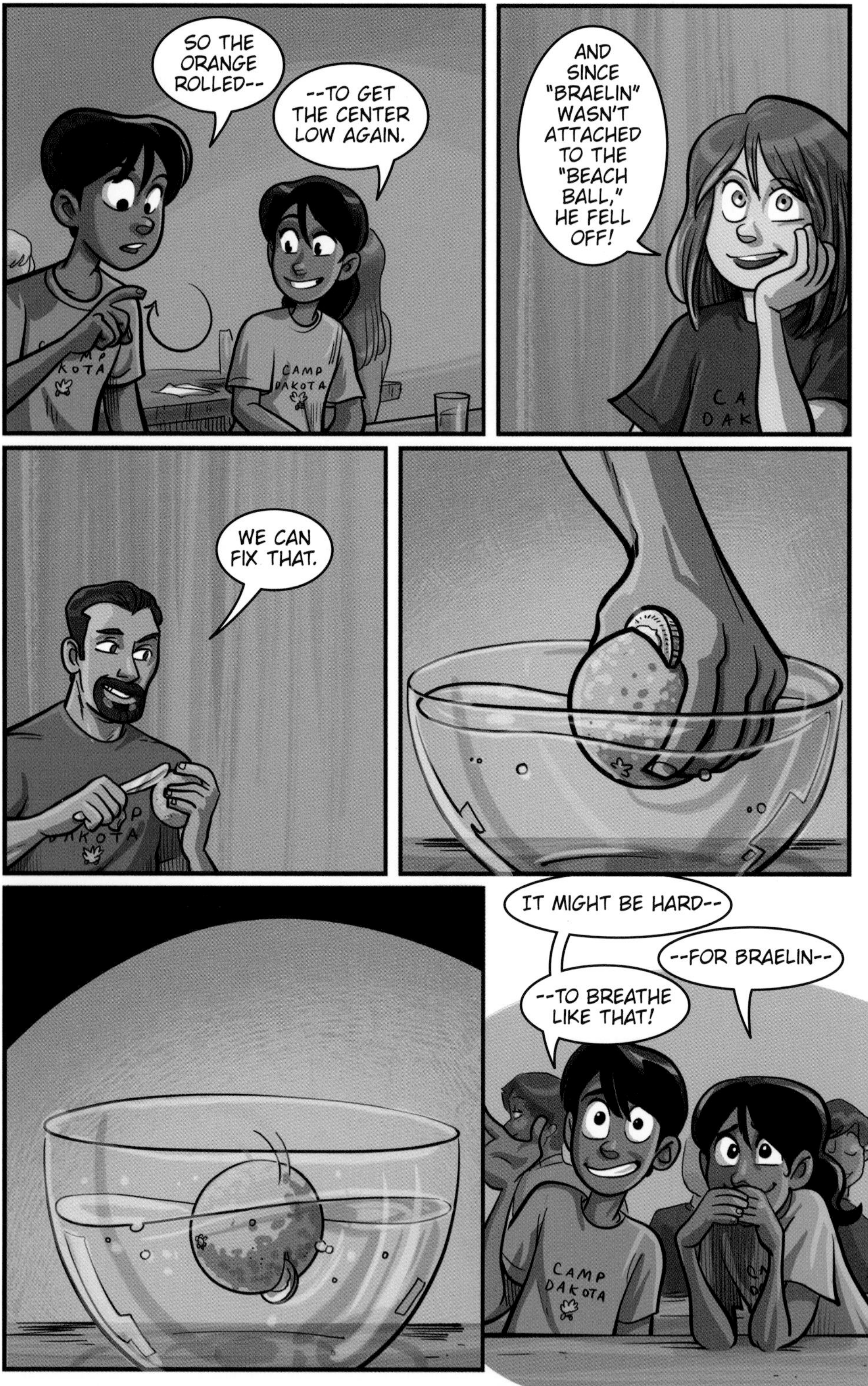
SO THE ORANGE ROLLED--
--TO GET THE CENTER LOW AGAIN.
CAMP DAKOTA
AND SINCE "BRAELIN" WASN'T ATTACHED TO THE "BEACH BALL," HE FELL OFF!
WE CAN FIX THAT.
IT MIGHT BE HARD--
--FOR BRAELIN--
--TO BREATHE LIKE THAT!
CAMP DAKOTA

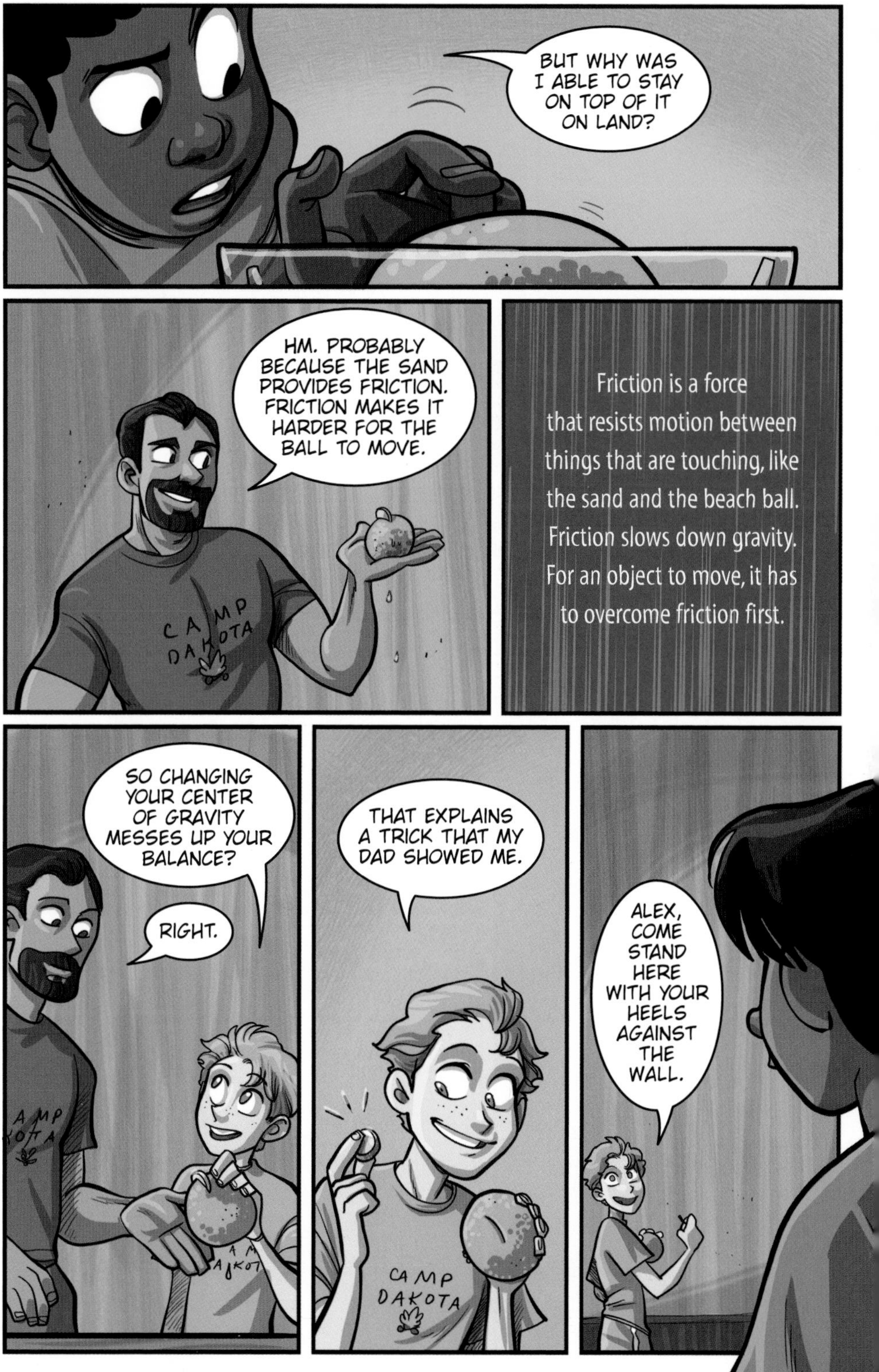

BUT WHY WAS I ABLE TO STAY ON TOP OF IT ON LAND?
HM. PROBABLY BECAUSE THE SAND PROVIDES FRICTION. FRICTION MAKES IT HARDER FOR THE BALL TO MOVE.
CAMP DAKOTA
Friction is a force that resists motion between things that are touching, like the sand and the beach ball. Friction slows down gravity. For an object to move, it has to overcome friction first.
SO CHANGING YOUR CENTER OF GRAVITY MESSES UP YOUR BALANCE?
RIGHT.
THAT EXPLAINS A TRICK THAT MY DAD SHOWED ME.
CAMP DAKOTA
ALEX, COME STAND HERE WITH YOUR HEELS AGAINST THE WALL.

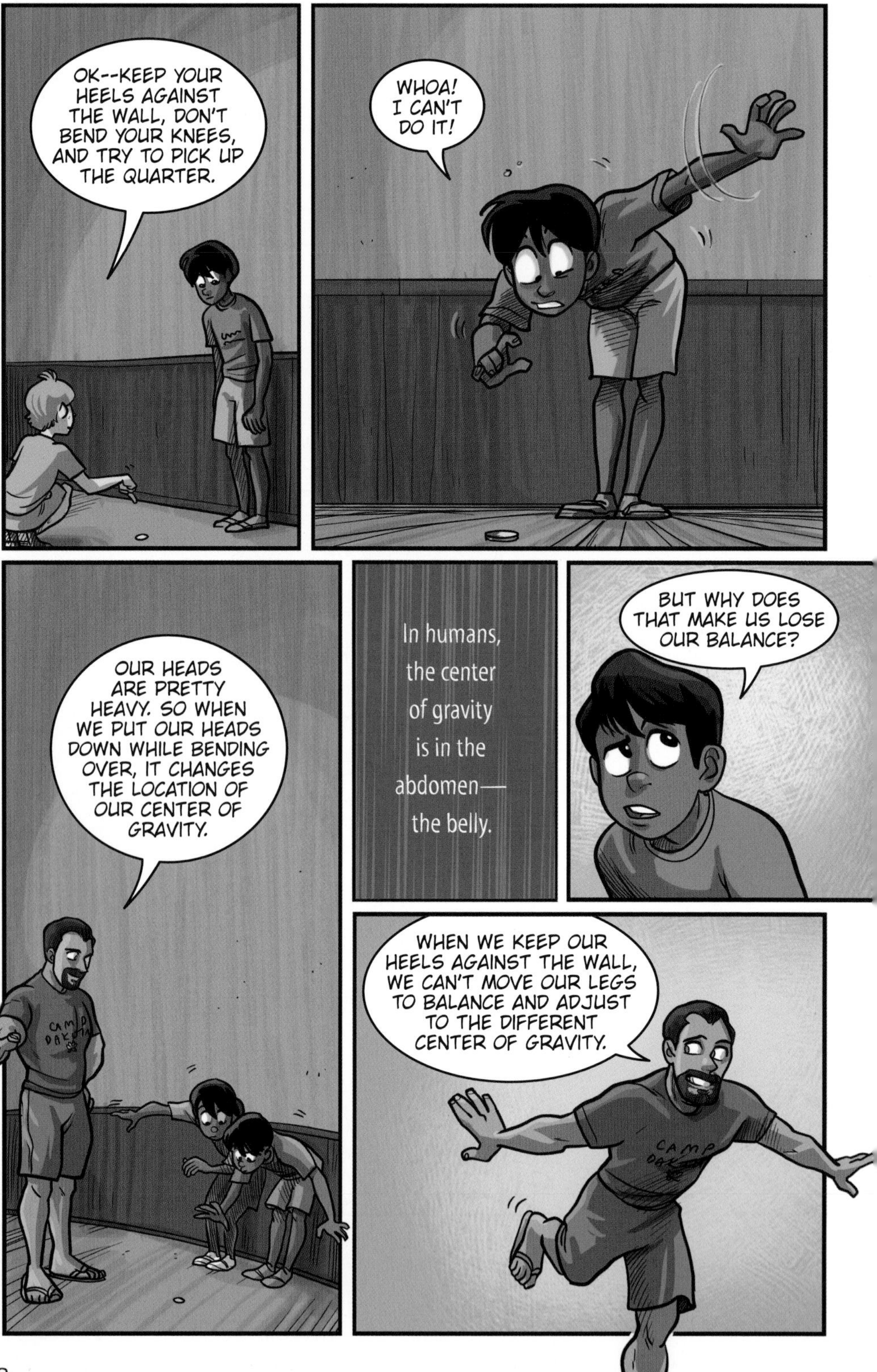
OK--KEEP YOUR HEELS AGAINST THE WALL, DON'T BEND YOUR KNEES, AND TRY TO PICK UP THE QUARTER.
WHOA! I CAN'T DO IT!
OUR HEADS ARE PRETTY HEAVY. SO WHEN WE PUT OUR HEADS DOWN WHILE BENDING OVER, IT CHANGES THE LOCATION OF OUR CENTER OF GRAVITY.
In humans, the center of gravity is in the abdomen—the belly.
BUT WHY DOES THAT MAKE US LOSE OUR BALANCE?
WHEN WE KEEP OUR HEELS AGAINST THE WALL, WE CAN'T MOVE OUR LEGS TO BALANCE AND ADJUST TO THE DIFFERENT CENTER OF GRAVITY.

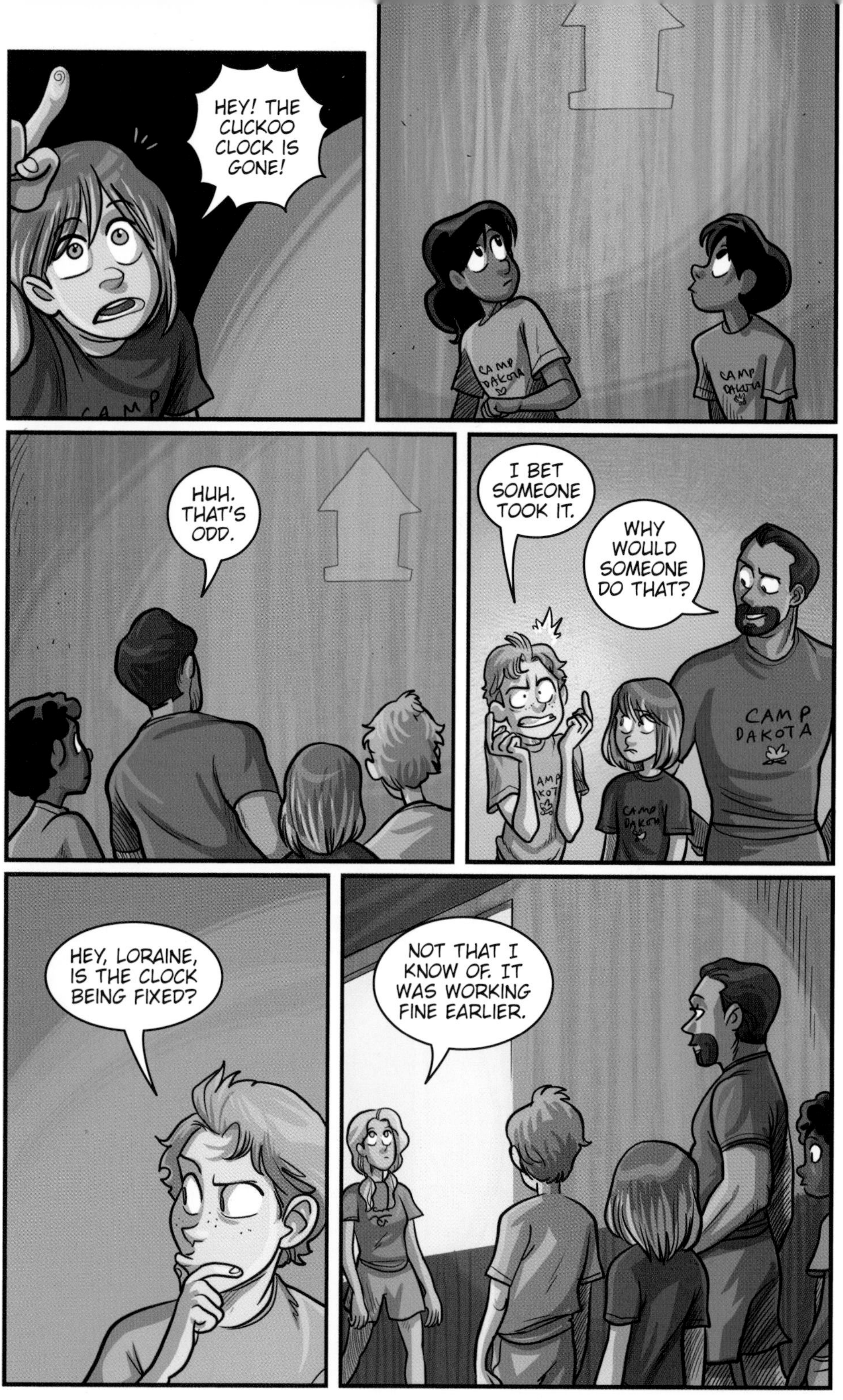
HEY! THE CUCKOO CLOCK IS GONE!
CAMP
CAMP DAKOTA
CAMP DAKOTA
HUH. THAT'S ODD.
I BET SOMEONE TOOK IT.
WHY WOULD SOMEONE DO THAT?
CAMP DAKOTA
CAMP DAKOTA
HEY, LORAINE, IS THE CLOCK BEING FIXED?
NOT THAT I KNOW OF. IT WAS WORKING FINE EARLIER.

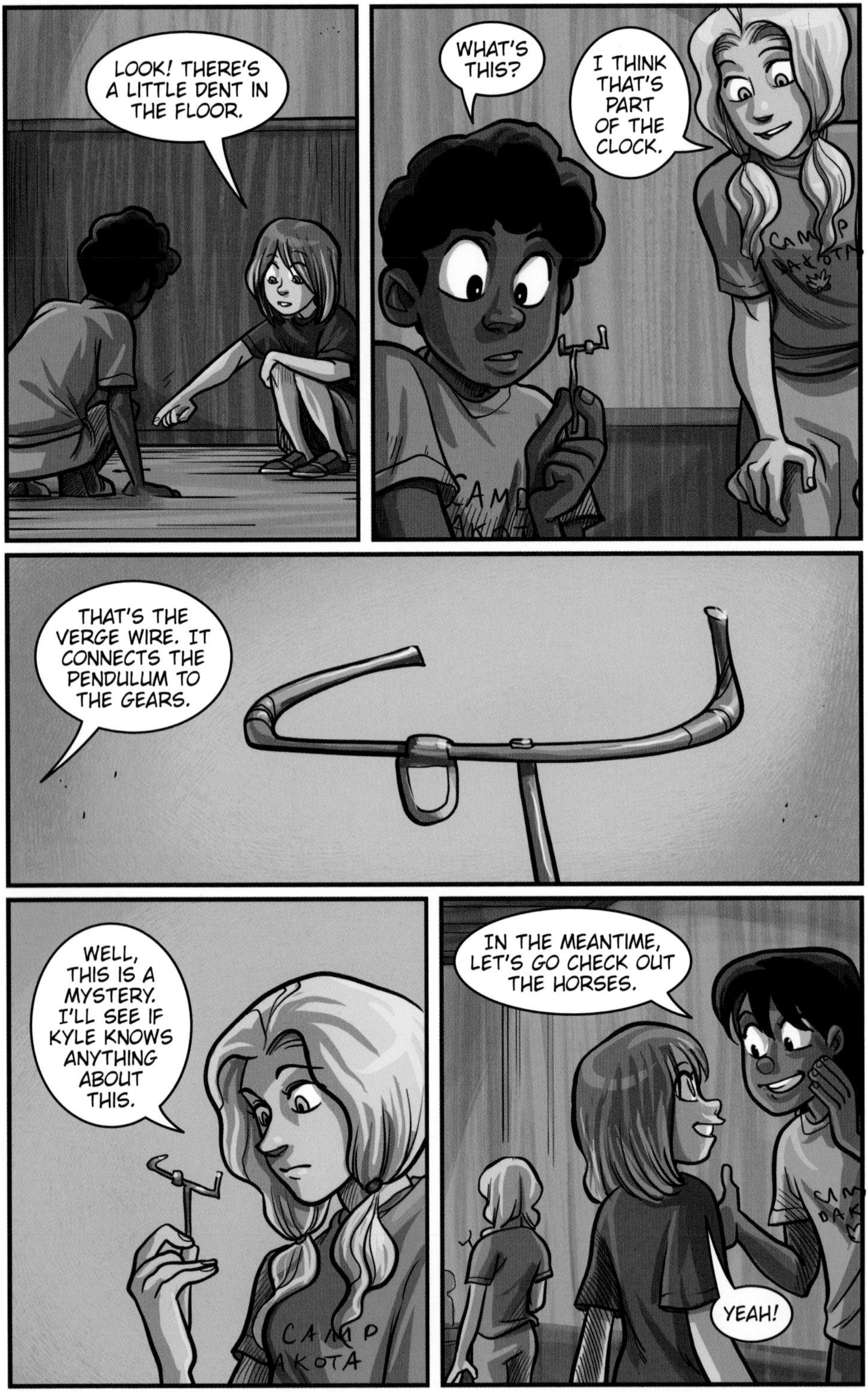
LOOK! THERE'S A LITTLE DENT IN THE FLOOR.
WHAT'S THIS?
I THINK THAT'S PART OF THE CLOCK.
THAT'S THE VERGE WIRE. IT CONNECTS THE PENDULUM TO THE GEARS.
WELL, THIS IS A MYSTERY. I'LL SEE IF KYLE KNOWS ANYTHING ABOUT THIS.
IN THE MEANTIME, LET'S GO CHECK OUT THE HORSES.
YEAH!

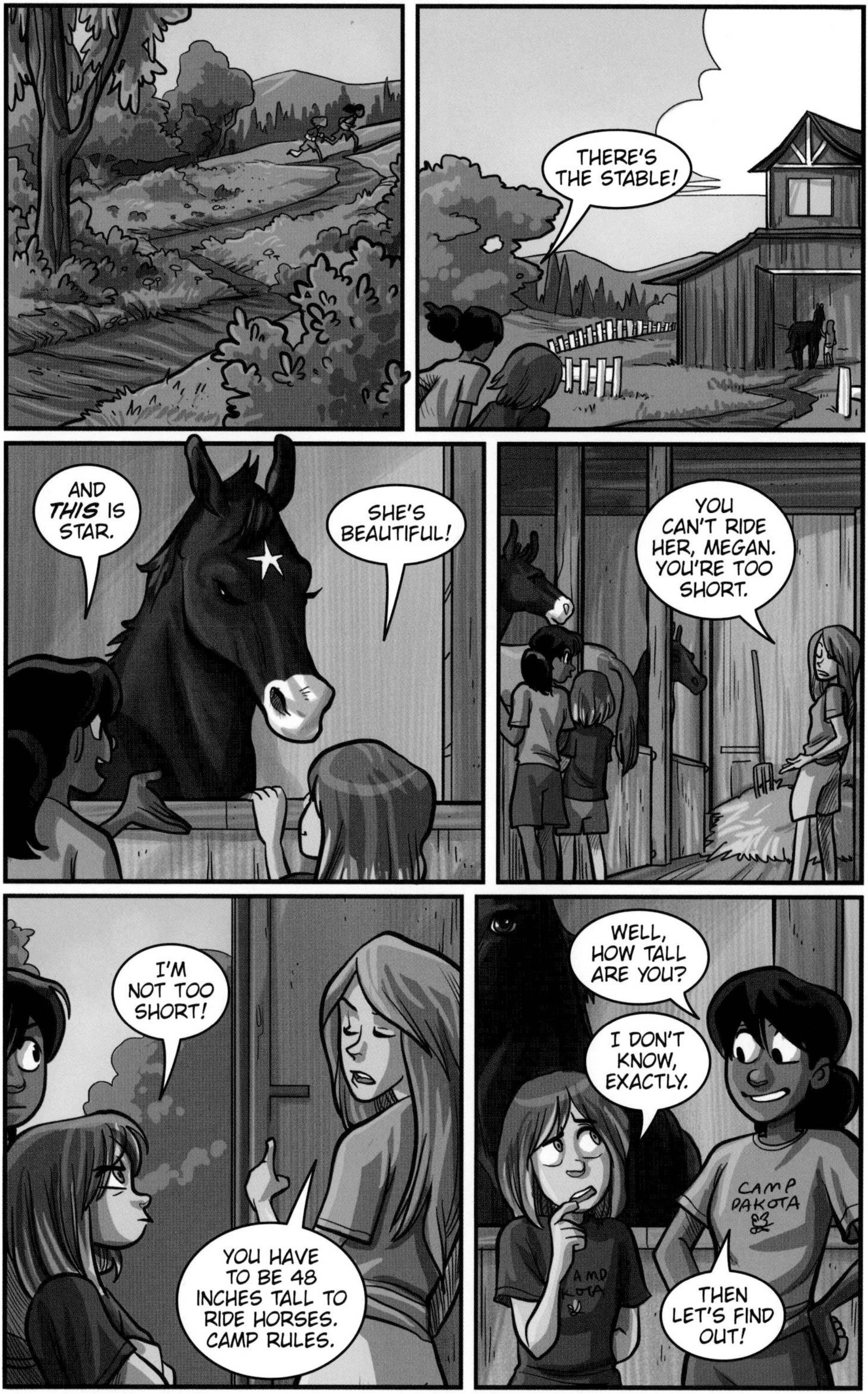
THERE'S THE STABLE!
AND *THIS* IS STAR.
SHE'S BEAUTIFUL!
YOU CAN'T RIDE HER, MEGAN. YOU'RE TOO SHORT.
I'M NOT TOO SHORT!
YOU HAVE TO BE 48 INCHES TALL TO RIDE HORSES. CAMP RULES.
WELL, HOW TALL ARE YOU?
I DON'T KNOW, EXACTLY.
THEN LET'S FIND OUT!
CAMP DAKOTA

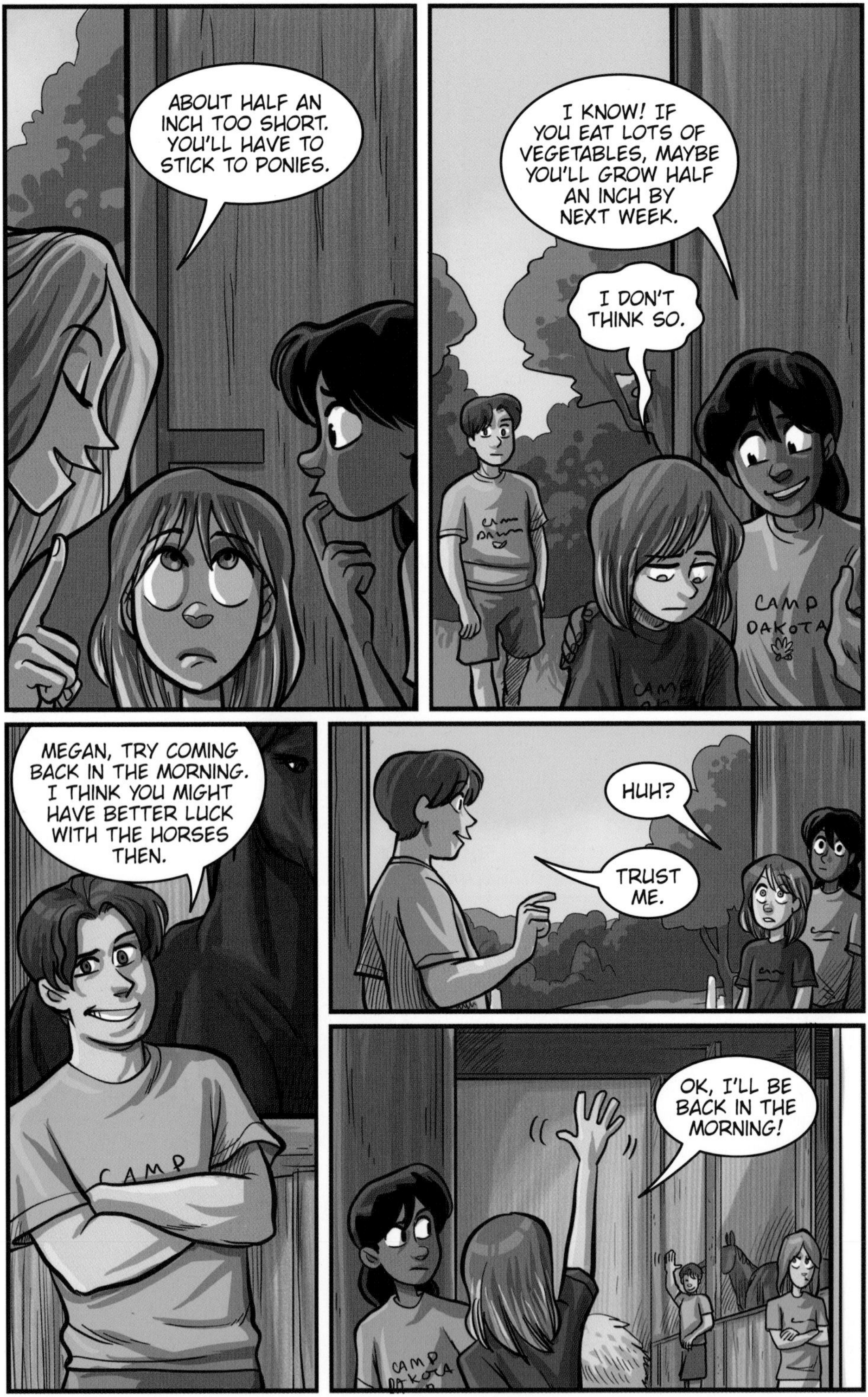
ABOUT HALF AN INCH TOO SHORT. YOU'LL HAVE TO STICK TO PONIES.
I KNOW! IF YOU EAT LOTS OF VEGETABLES, MAYBE YOU'LL GROW HALF AN INCH BY NEXT WEEK.
I DON'T THINK SO.
CAMP DAKOTA
MEGAN, TRY COMING BACK IN THE MORNING. I THINK YOU MIGHT HAVE BETTER LUCK WITH THE HORSES THEN.
HUH?
TRUST ME.
OK, I'LL BE BACK IN THE MORNING!

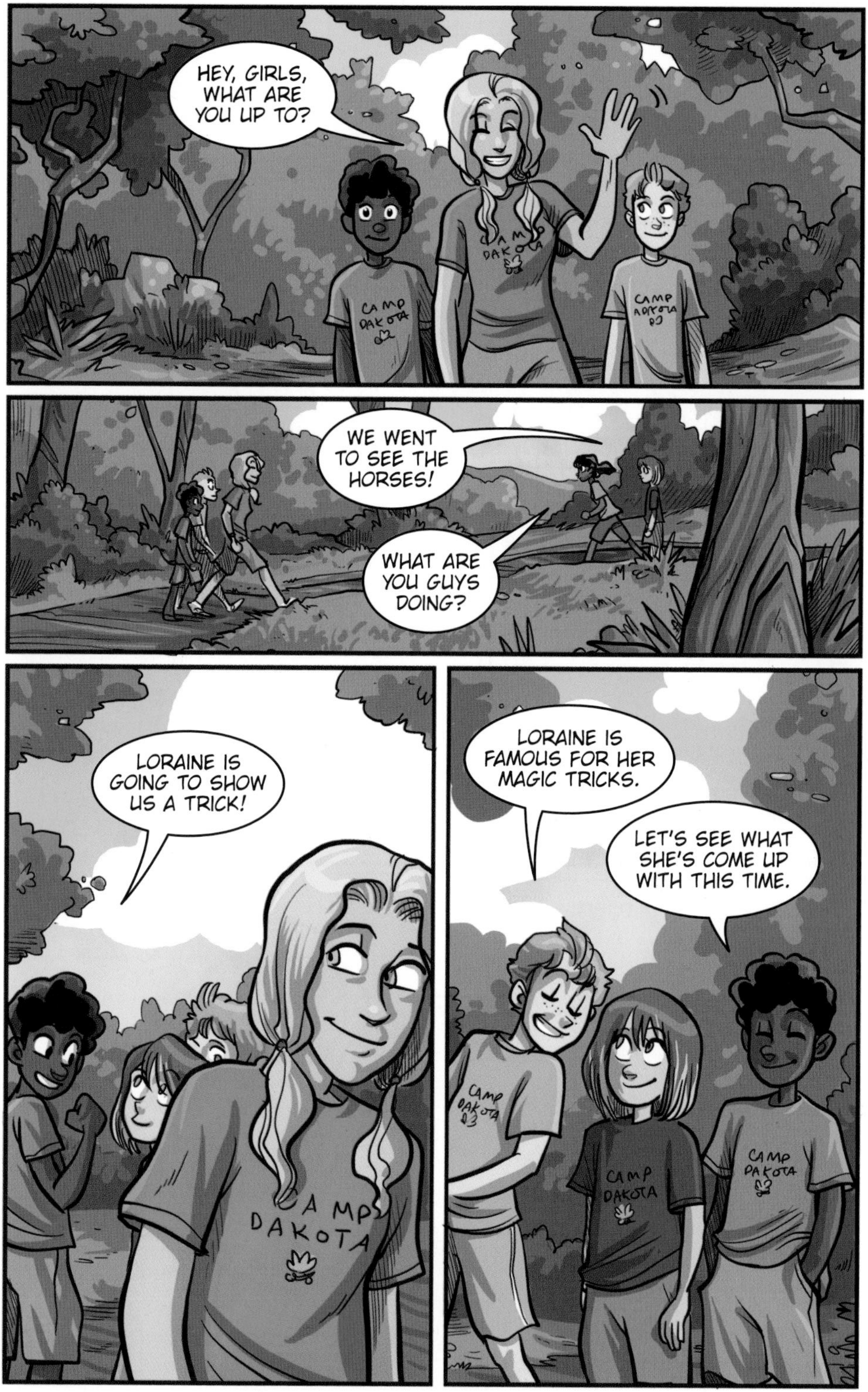
HEY, GIRLS, WHAT ARE YOU UP TO?
CAMP DAKOTA
WE WENT TO SEE THE HORSES!
WHAT ARE YOU GUYS DOING?
LORAINE IS GOING TO SHOW US A TRICK!
CAMP DAKOTA
LORAINE IS FAMOUS FOR HER MAGIC TRICKS.
LET'S SEE WHAT SHE'S COME UP WITH THIS TIME.
CAMP DAKOTA

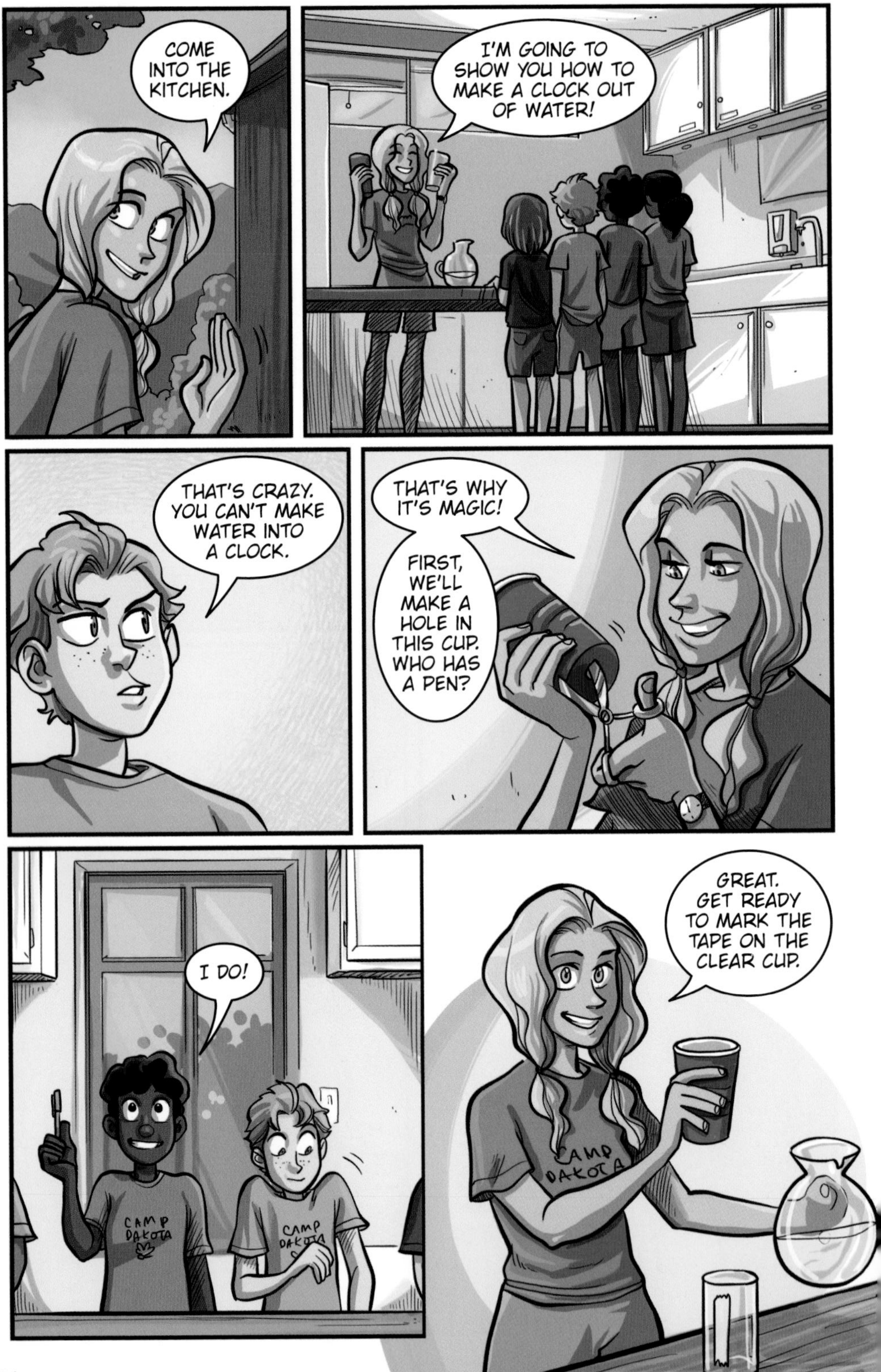
COME INTO THE KITCHEN.
I'M GOING TO SHOW YOU HOW TO MAKE A CLOCK OUT OF WATER!
THAT'S CRAZY. YOU CAN'T MAKE WATER INTO A CLOCK.
THAT'S WHY IT'S MAGIC!
FIRST, WE'LL MAKE A HOLE IN THIS CUP. WHO HAS A PEN?
I DO!
CAMP DAKOTA
CAMP DAKOTA
GREAT. GET READY TO MARK THE TAPE ON THE CLEAR CUP.
CAMP DAKOTA

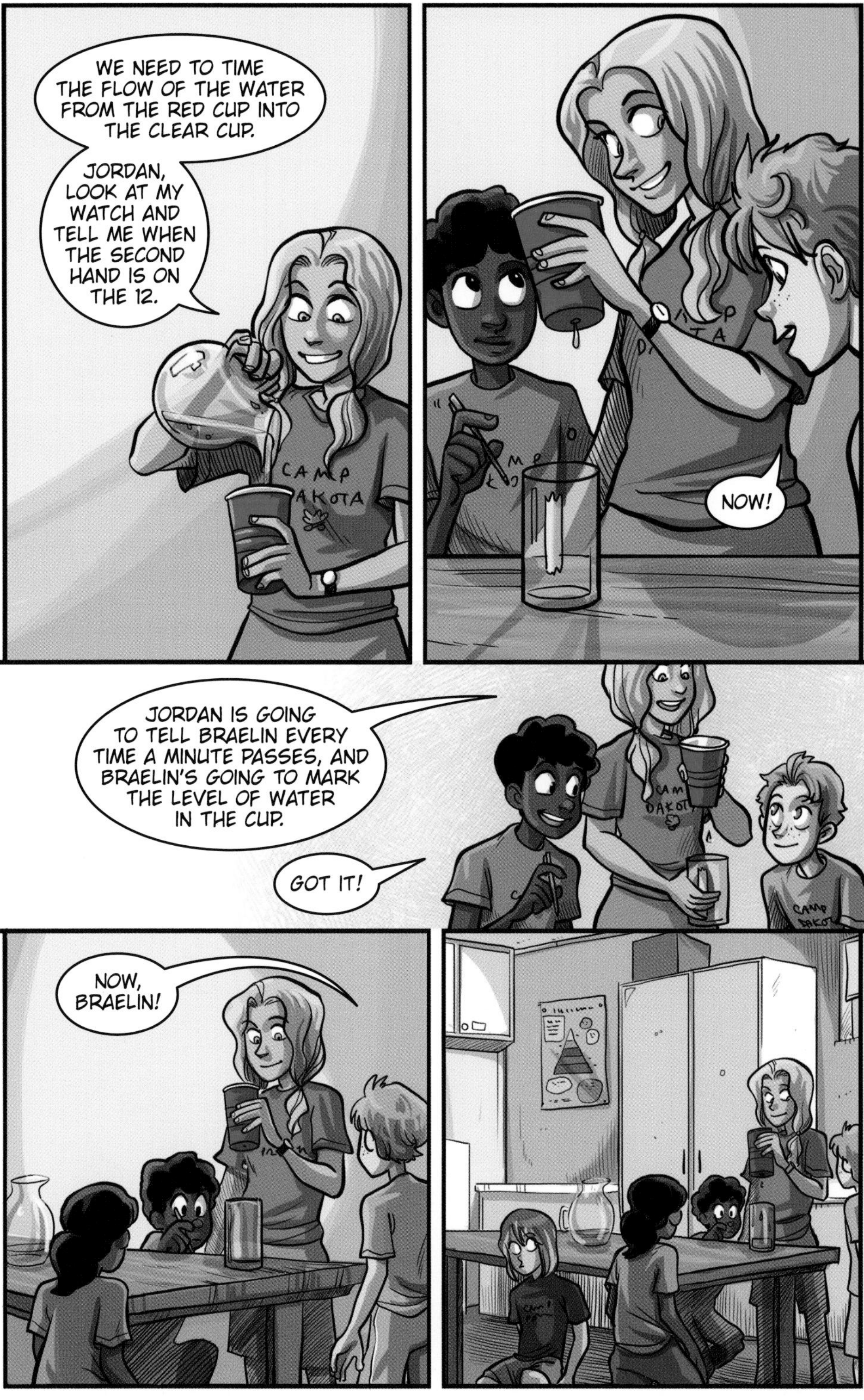
WE NEED TO TIME THE FLOW OF THE WATER FROM THE RED CUP INTO THE CLEAR CUP.
JORDAN, LOOK AT MY WATCH AND TELL ME WHEN THE SECOND HAND IS ON THE 12.
CAMP DAKOTA
NOW!
JORDAN IS GOING TO TELL BRAELIN EVERY TIME A MINUTE PASSES, AND BRAELIN'S GOING TO MARK THE LEVEL OF WATER IN THE CUP.
GOT IT!
NOW, BRAELIN!

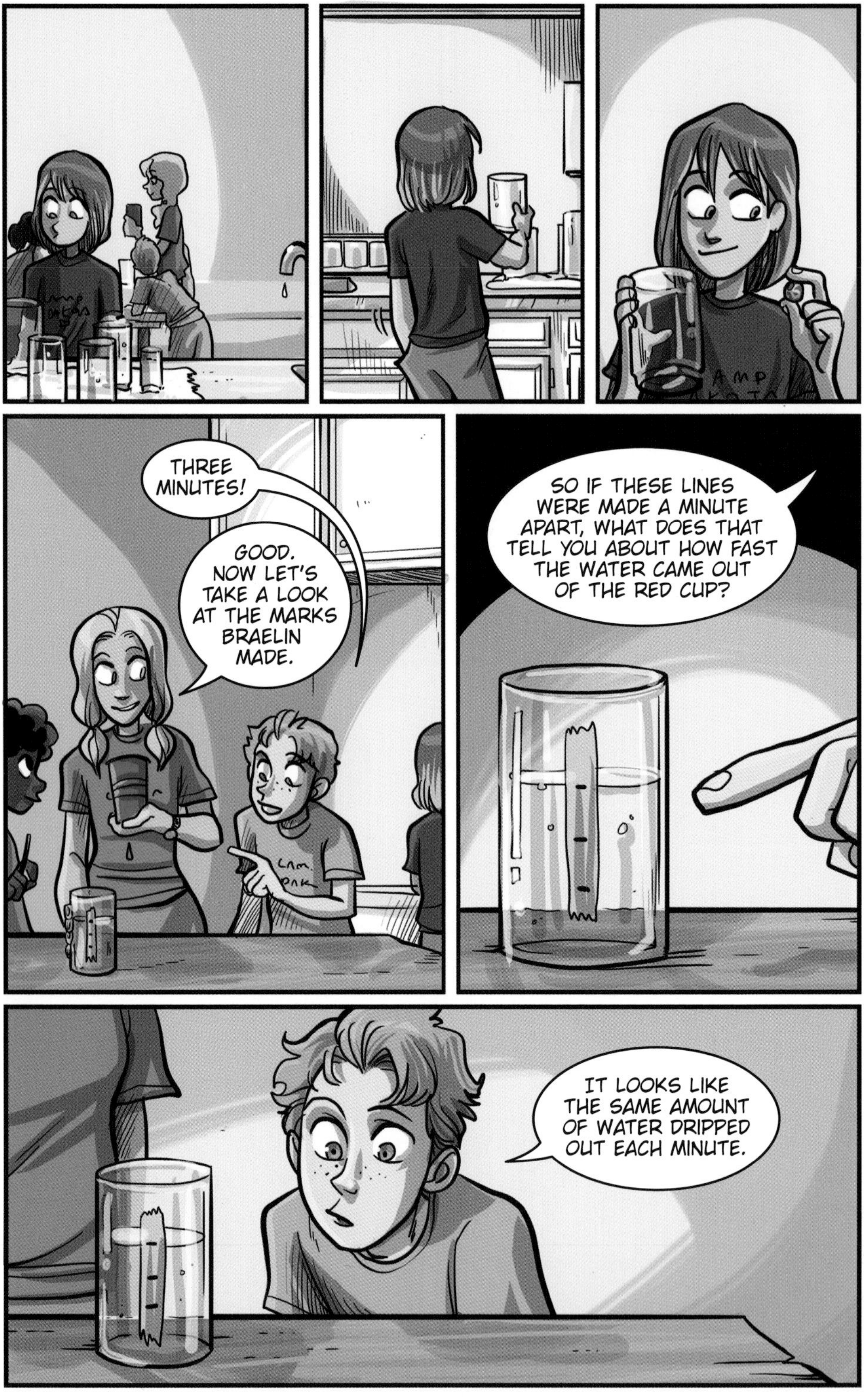
THREE MINUTES!
GOOD. NOW LET'S TAKE A LOOK AT THE MARKS BRAELIN MADE.
SO IF THESE LINES WERE MADE A MINUTE APART, WHAT DOES THAT TELL YOU ABOUT HOW FAST THE WATER CAME OUT OF THE RED CUP?
IT LOOKS LIKE THE SAME AMOUNT OF WATER DRIPPED OUT EACH MINUTE.

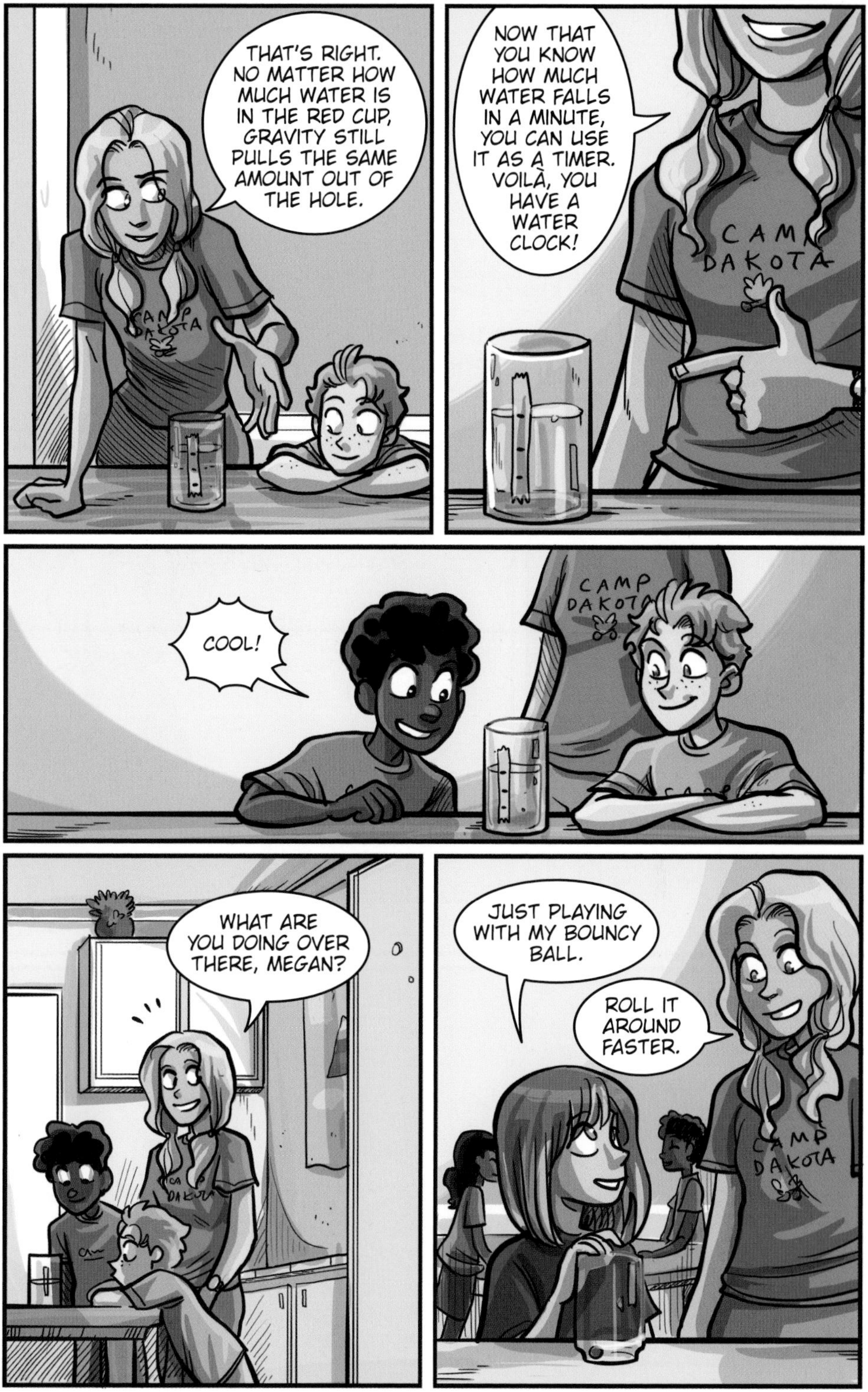
THAT'S RIGHT. NO MATTER HOW MUCH WATER IS IN THE RED CUP, GRAVITY STILL PULLS THE SAME AMOUNT OUT OF THE HOLE.
NOW THAT YOU KNOW HOW MUCH WATER FALLS IN A MINUTE, YOU CAN USE IT AS A TIMER. VOILÀ, YOU HAVE A WATER CLOCK!
CAMP DAKOTA
COOL!
WHAT ARE YOU DOING OVER THERE, MEGAN?
JUST PLAYING WITH MY BOUNCY BALL.
ROLL IT AROUND FASTER.
CAMP DAKOTA

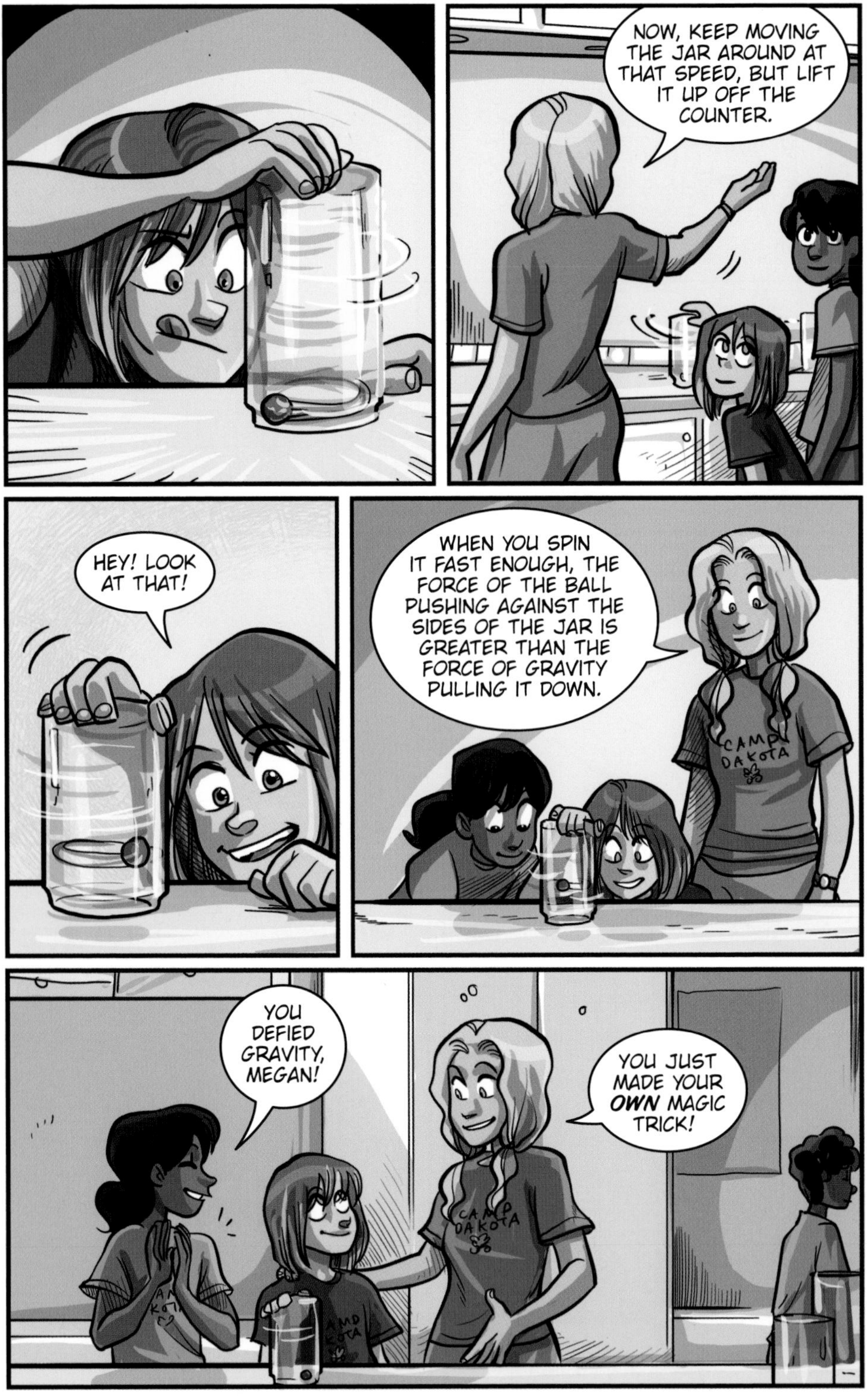
NOW, KEEP MOVING THE JAR AROUND AT THAT SPEED, BUT LIFT IT UP OFF THE COUNTER.
HEY! LOOK AT THAT!
WHEN YOU SPIN IT FAST ENOUGH, THE FORCE OF THE BALL PUSHING AGAINST THE SIDES OF THE JAR IS GREATER THAN THE FORCE OF GRAVITY PULLING IT DOWN.
YOU DEFIED GRAVITY, MEGAN!
YOU JUST MADE YOUR ***OWN*** MAGIC TRICK!

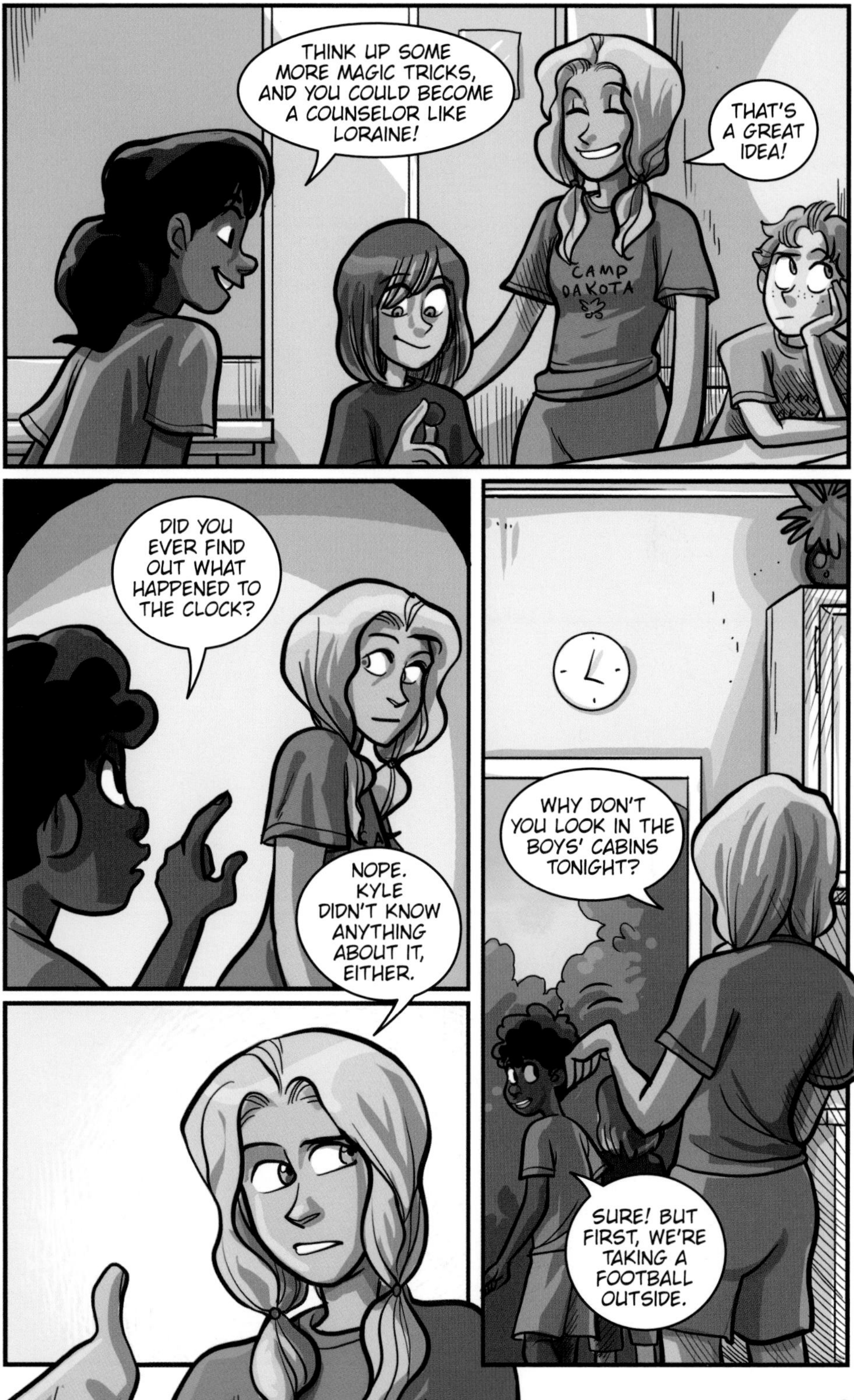
THINK UP SOME MORE MAGIC TRICKS, AND YOU COULD BECOME A COUNSELOR LIKE LORAINE!
THAT'S A GREAT IDEA!
CAMP DAKOTA
DID YOU EVER FIND OUT WHAT HAPPENED TO THE CLOCK?
NOPE. KYLE DIDN'T KNOW ANYTHING ABOUT IT, EITHER.
WHY DON'T YOU LOOK IN THE BOYS' CABINS TONIGHT?
SURE! BUT FIRST, WE'RE TAKING A FOOTBALL OUTSIDE.

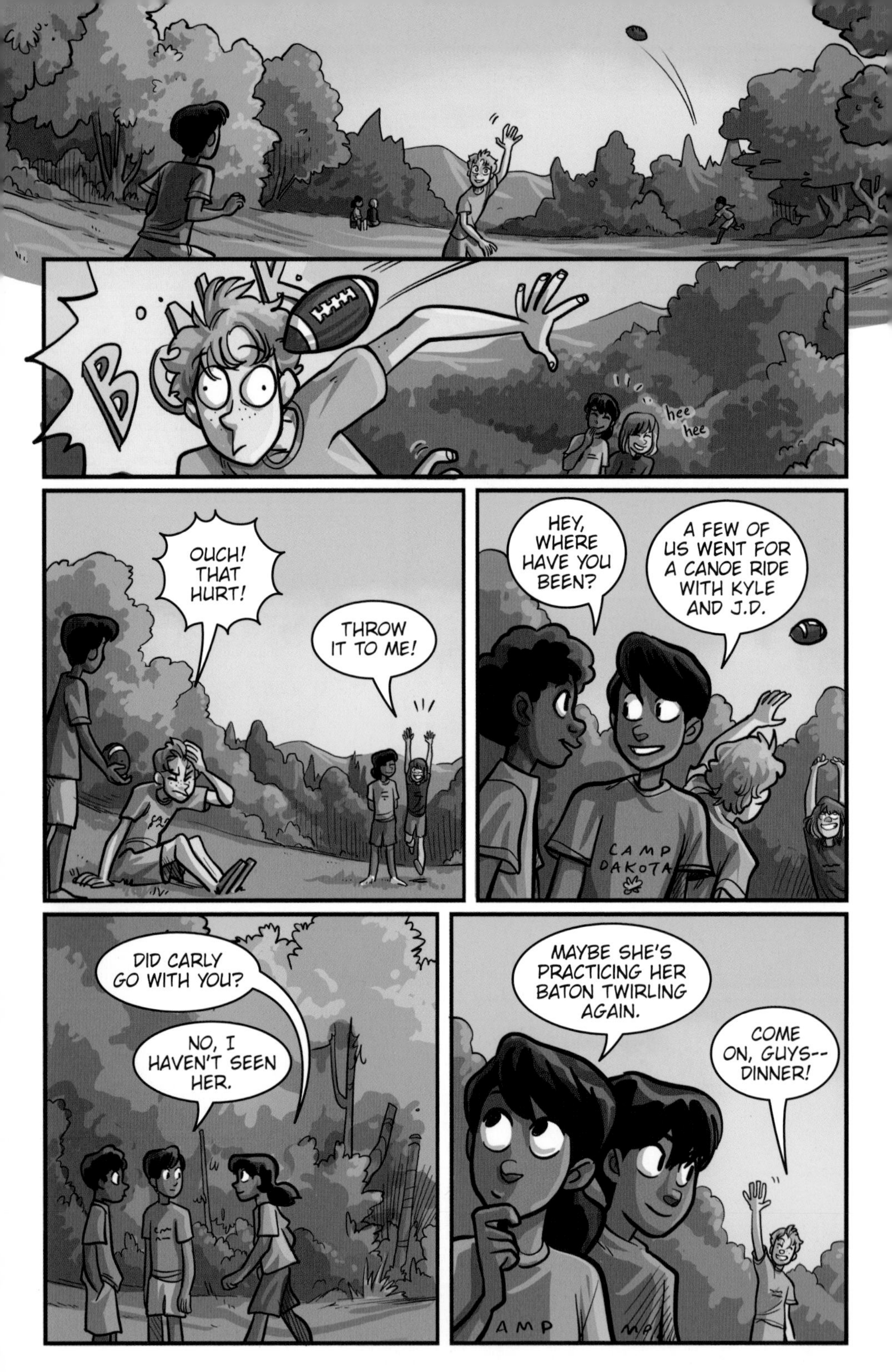
BOINK!
hee
hee
OUCH! THAT HURT!
THROW IT TO ME!
HEY, WHERE HAVE YOU BEEN?
A FEW OF US WENT FOR A CANOE RIDE WITH KYLE AND J.D.
CAMP DAKOTA
DID CARLY GO WITH YOU?
NO, I HAVEN'T SEEN HER.
MAYBE SHE'S PRACTICING HER BATON TWIRLING AGAIN.
COME ON, GUYS-- DINNER!

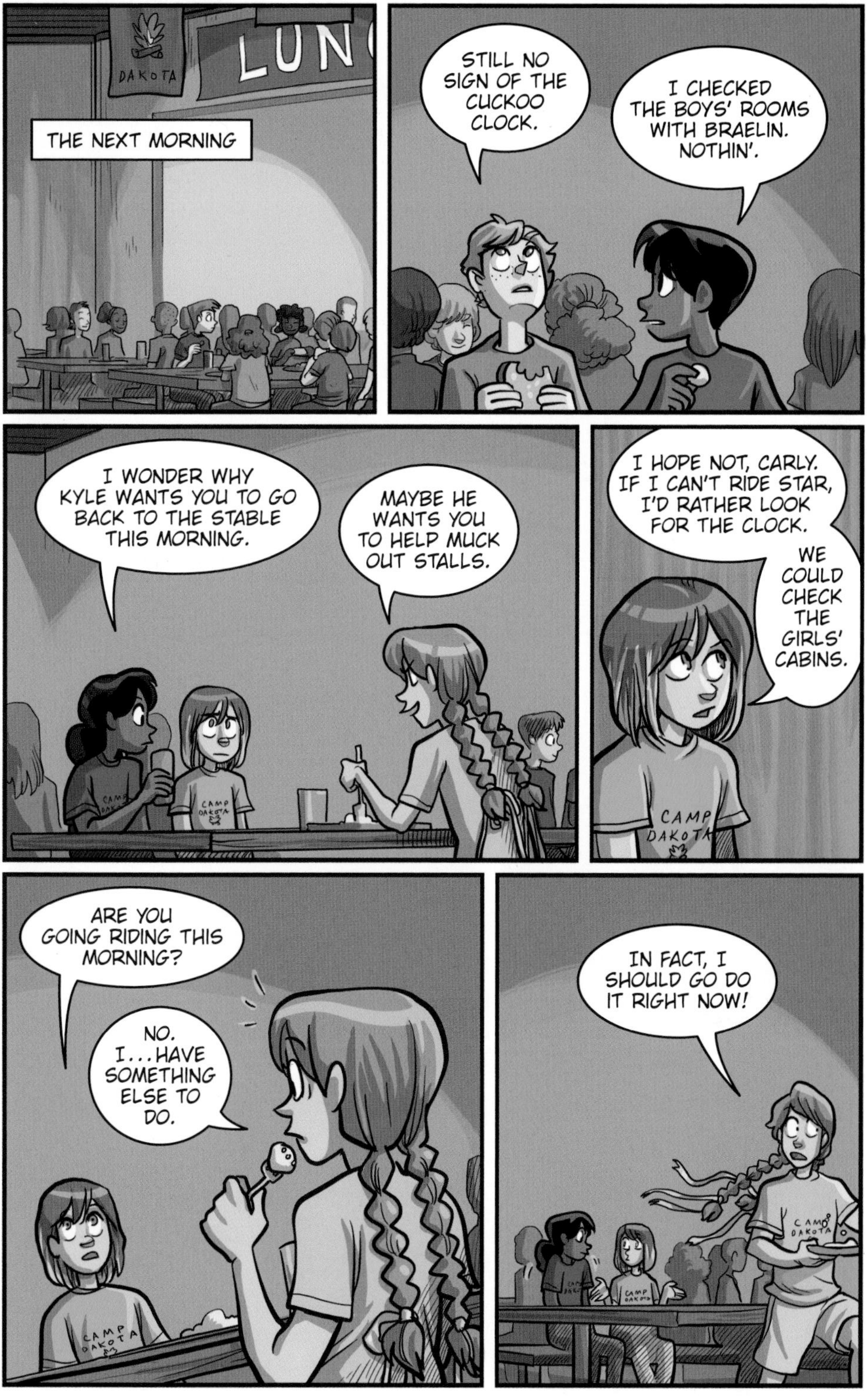
LUN
DAKOTA
THE NEXT MORNING
STILL NO SIGN OF THE CUCKOO CLOCK.
I CHECKED THE BOYS' ROOMS WITH BRAELIN. NOTHIN'.
I WONDER WHY KYLE WANTS YOU TO GO BACK TO THE STABLE THIS MORNING.
MAYBE HE WANTS YOU TO HELP MUCK OUT STALLS.
CAMP DAKOTA
I HOPE NOT, CARLY. IF I CAN'T RIDE STAR, I'D RATHER LOOK FOR THE CLOCK.
WE COULD CHECK THE GIRLS' CABINS.
ARE YOU GOING RIDING THIS MORNING?
NO. I...HAVE SOMETHING ELSE TO DO.
IN FACT, I SHOULD GO DO IT RIGHT NOW!

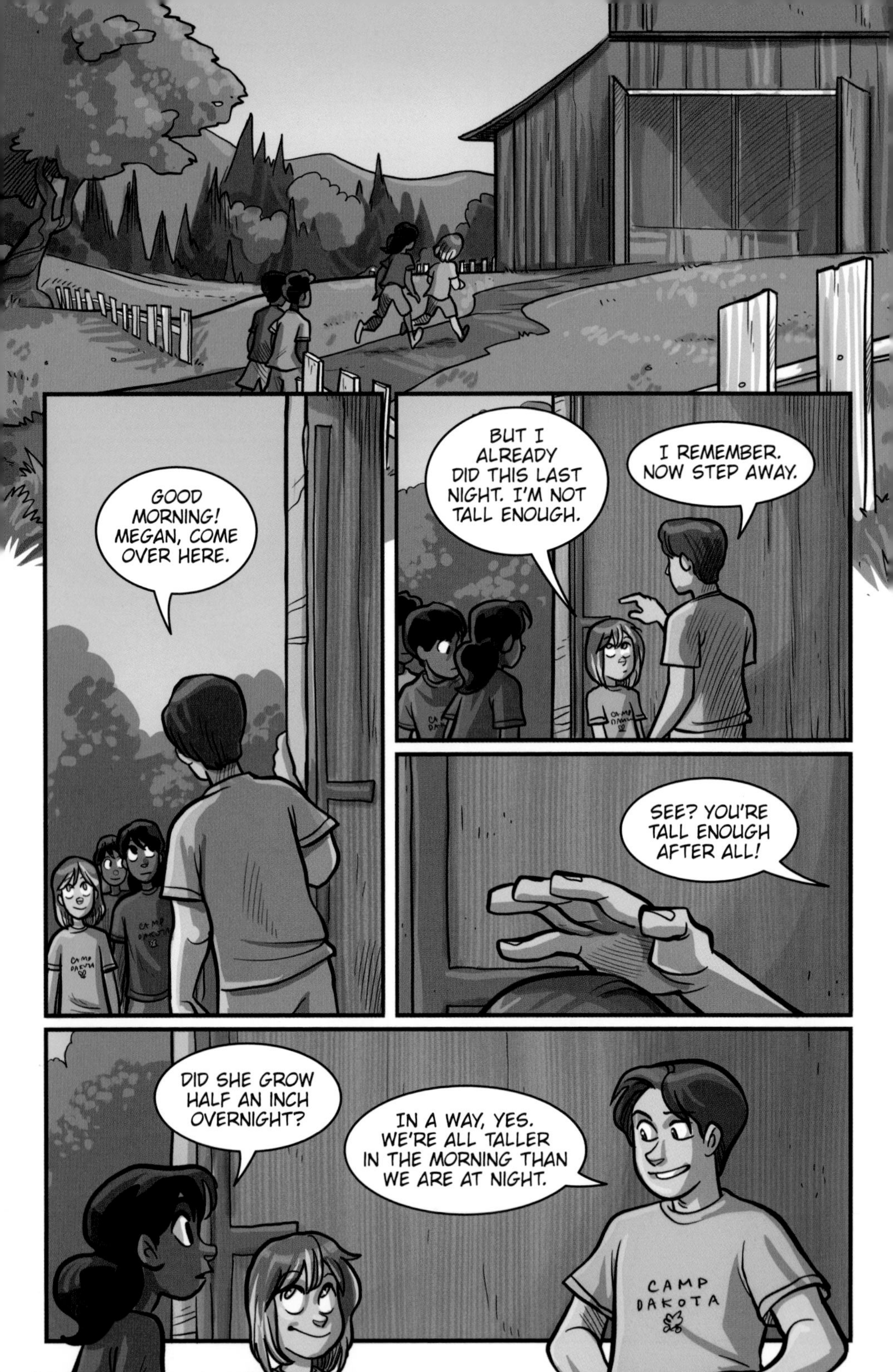
GOOD MORNING! MEGAN, COME OVER HERE.
BUT I ALREADY DID THIS LAST NIGHT. I'M NOT TALL ENOUGH.
I REMEMBER. NOW STEP AWAY.
SEE? YOU'RE TALL ENOUGH AFTER ALL!
DID SHE GROW HALF AN INCH OVERNIGHT?
IN A WAY, YES. WE'RE ALL TALLER IN THE MORNING THAN WE ARE AT NIGHT.
CAMP DAKOTA

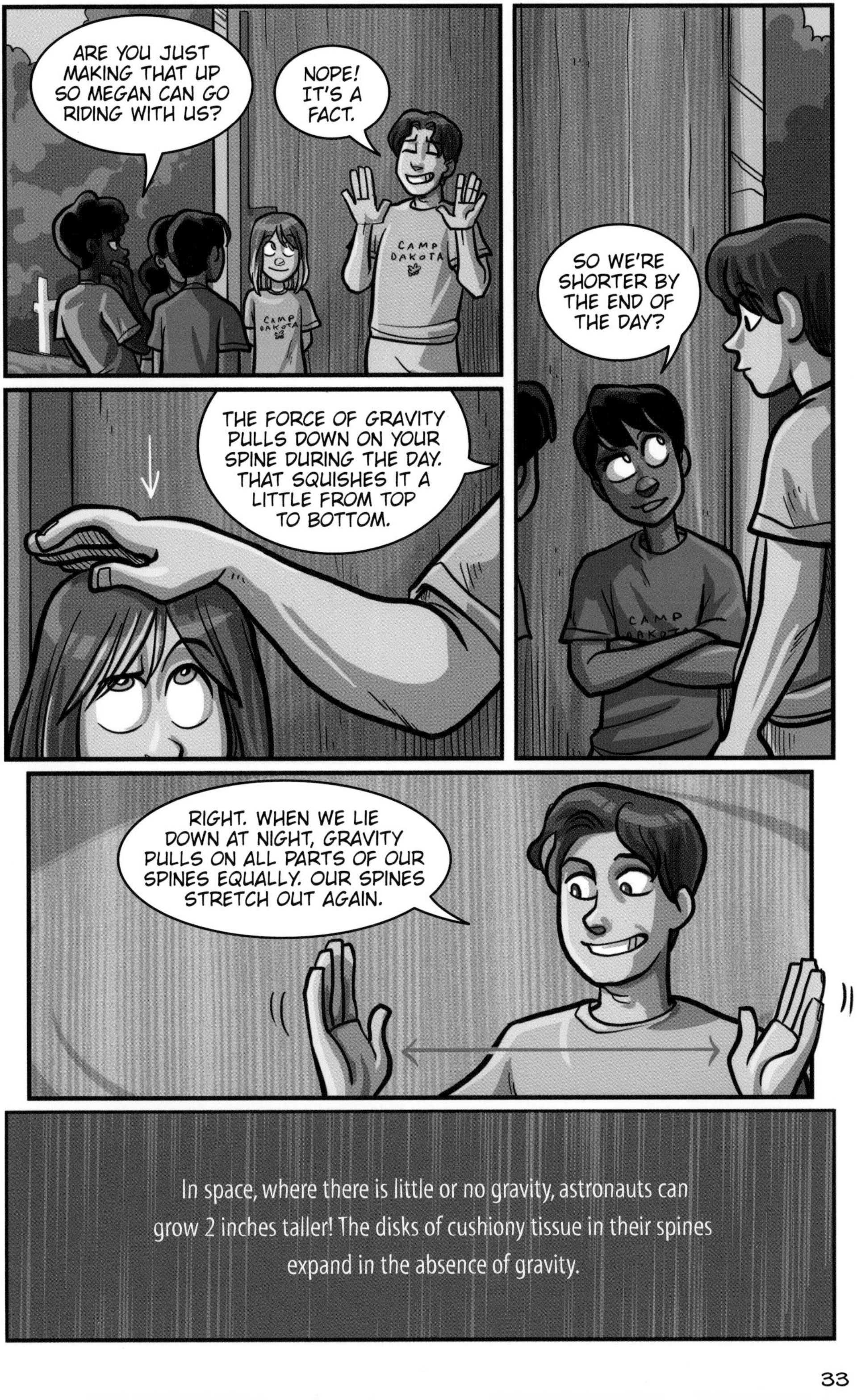
ARE YOU JUST MAKING THAT UP SO MEGAN CAN GO RIDING WITH US?
NOPE! IT'S A FACT.
CAMP DAKOTA
SO WE'RE SHORTER BY THE END OF THE DAY?
THE FORCE OF GRAVITY PULLS DOWN ON YOUR SPINE DURING THE DAY. THAT SQUISHES IT A LITTLE FROM TOP TO BOTTOM.
RIGHT. WHEN WE LIE DOWN AT NIGHT, GRAVITY PULLS ON ALL PARTS OF OUR SPINES EQUALLY. OUR SPINES STRETCH OUT AGAIN.

In space, where there is little or no gravity, astronauts can grow 2 inches taller! The disks of cushiony tissue in their spines expand in the absence of gravity.

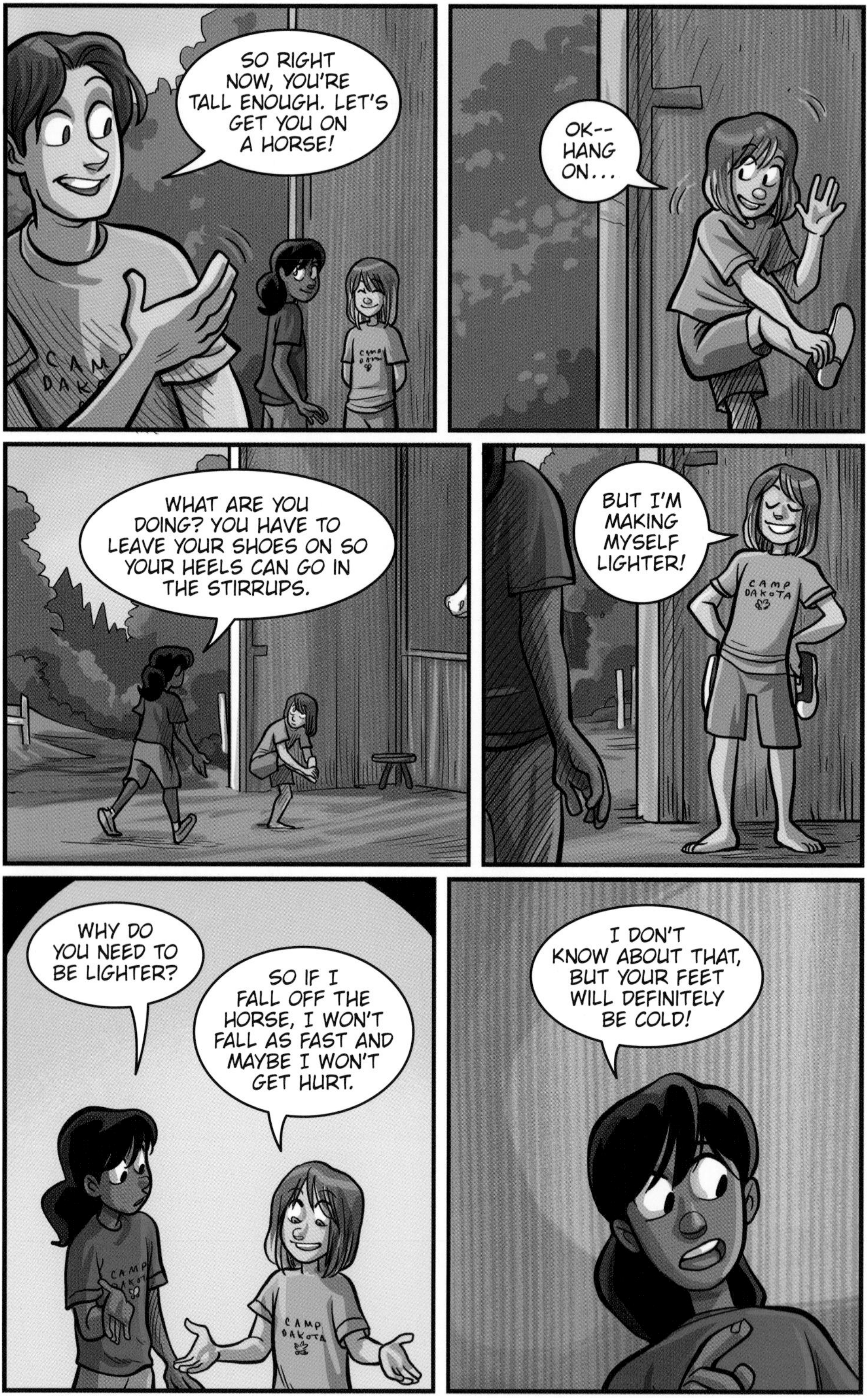
SO RIGHT NOW, YOU'RE TALL ENOUGH. LET'S GET YOU ON A HORSE!
CAMP DAKOTA
OK--HANG ON...
CAMP DAKOTA
WHAT ARE YOU DOING? YOU HAVE TO LEAVE YOUR SHOES ON SO YOUR HEELS CAN GO IN THE STIRRUPS.
BUT I'M MAKING MYSELF LIGHTER!
CAMP DAKOTA
WHY DO YOU NEED TO BE LIGHTER?
SO IF I FALL OFF THE HORSE, I WON'T FALL AS FAST AND MAYBE I WON'T GET HURT.
CAMP DAKOTA
CAMP DAKOTA
I DON'T KNOW ABOUT THAT, BUT YOUR FEET WILL DEFINITELY BE COLD!

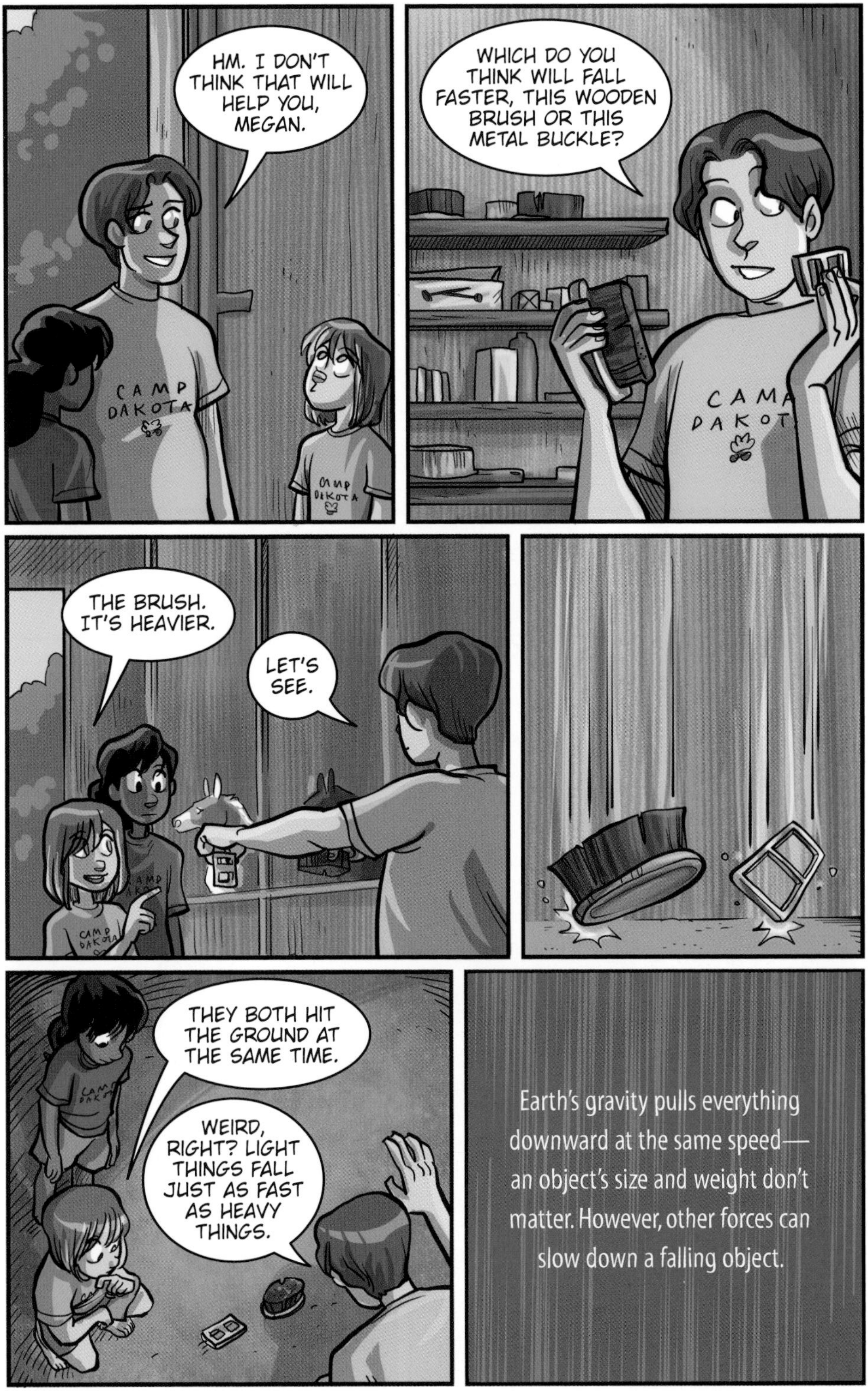

HM. I DON'T THINK THAT WILL HELP YOU, MEGAN.
WHICH DO YOU THINK WILL FALL FASTER, THIS WOODEN BRUSH OR THIS METAL BUCKLE?
THE BRUSH. IT'S HEAVIER.
LET'S SEE.
THEY BOTH HIT THE GROUND AT THE SAME TIME.
WEIRD, RIGHT? LIGHT THINGS FALL JUST AS FAST AS HEAVY THINGS.
Earth's gravity pulls everything downward at the same speed—an object's size and weight don't matter. However, other forces can slow down a falling object.

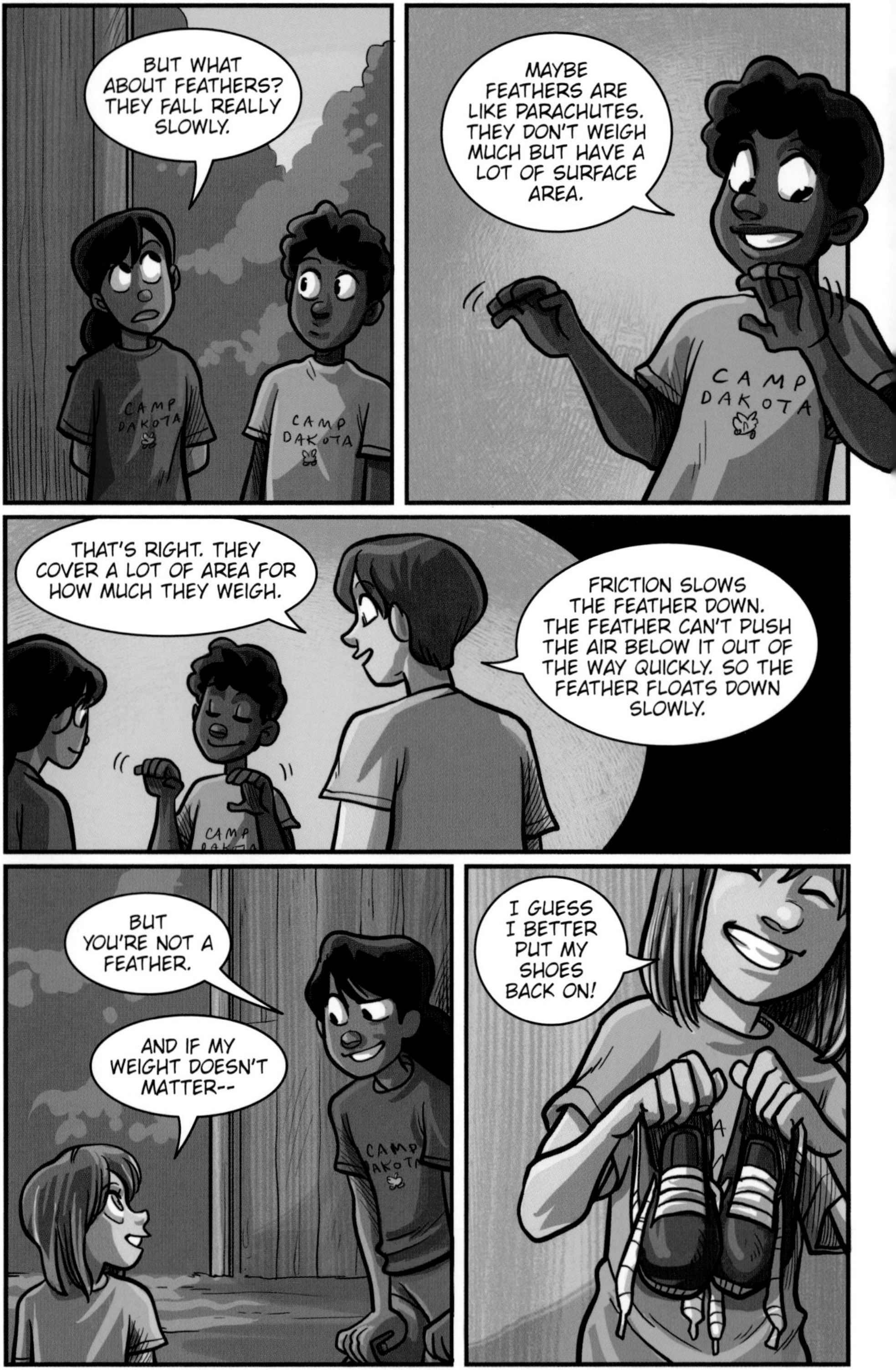

BUT WHAT ABOUT FEATHERS? THEY FALL REALLY SLOWLY.
CAMP DAKOTA
CAMP DAKOTA
MAYBE FEATHERS ARE LIKE PARACHUTES. THEY DON'T WEIGH MUCH BUT HAVE A LOT OF SURFACE AREA.
CAMP DAKOTA
THAT'S RIGHT. THEY COVER A LOT OF AREA FOR HOW MUCH THEY WEIGH.
FRICTION SLOWS THE FEATHER DOWN. THE FEATHER CAN'T PUSH THE AIR BELOW IT OUT OF THE WAY QUICKLY. SO THE FEATHER FLOATS DOWN SLOWLY.
BUT YOU'RE NOT A FEATHER.
AND IF MY WEIGHT DOESN'T MATTER--
CAMP DAKOTA
I GUESS I BETTER PUT MY SHOES BACK ON!

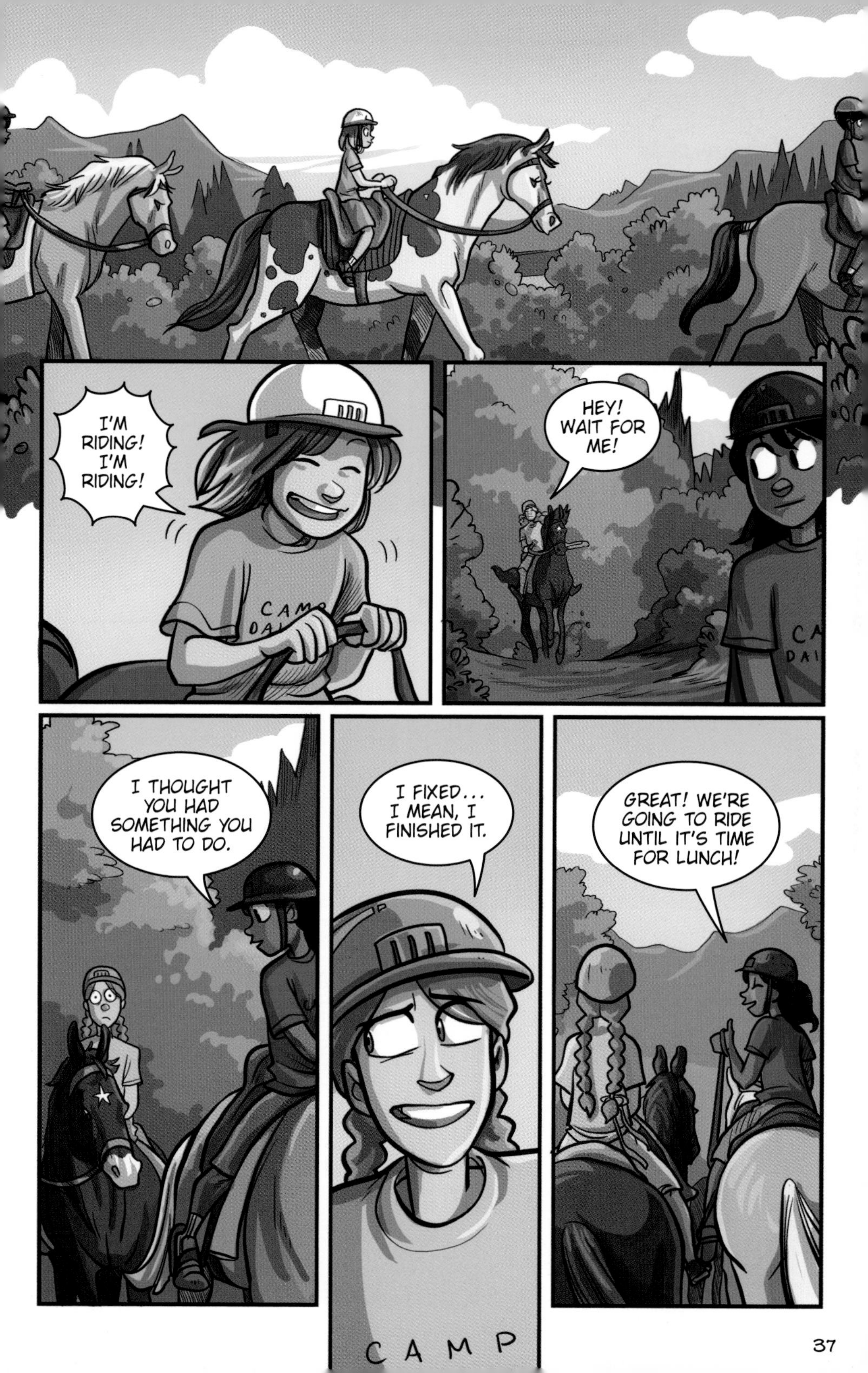
I'M RIDING! I'M RIDING!
CAMP DAI
HEY! WAIT FOR ME!
I THOUGHT YOU HAD SOMETHING YOU HAD TO DO.
I FIXED... I MEAN, I FINISHED IT.
GREAT! WE'RE GOING TO RIDE UNTIL IT'S TIME FOR LUNCH!
CAMP

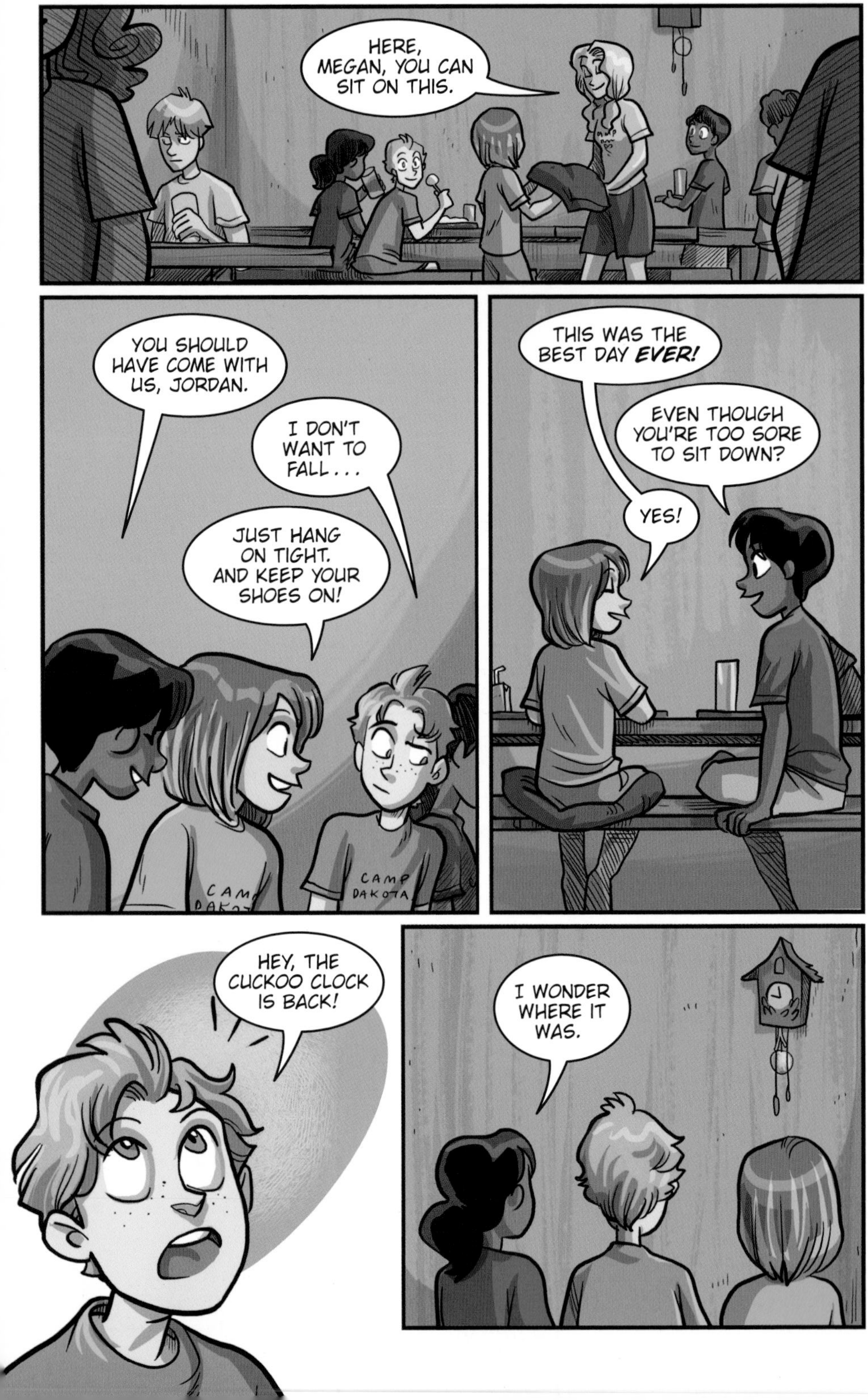
HERE, MEGAN, YOU CAN SIT ON THIS.
YOU SHOULD HAVE COME WITH US, JORDAN.
I DON'T WANT TO FALL . . .
JUST HANG ON TIGHT. AND KEEP YOUR SHOES ON!
CAMP DAKOTA
THIS WAS THE BEST DAY ***EVER!***
EVEN THOUGH YOU'RE TOO SORE TO SIT DOWN?
YES!
HEY, THE CUCKOO CLOCK IS BACK!
I WONDER WHERE IT WAS.

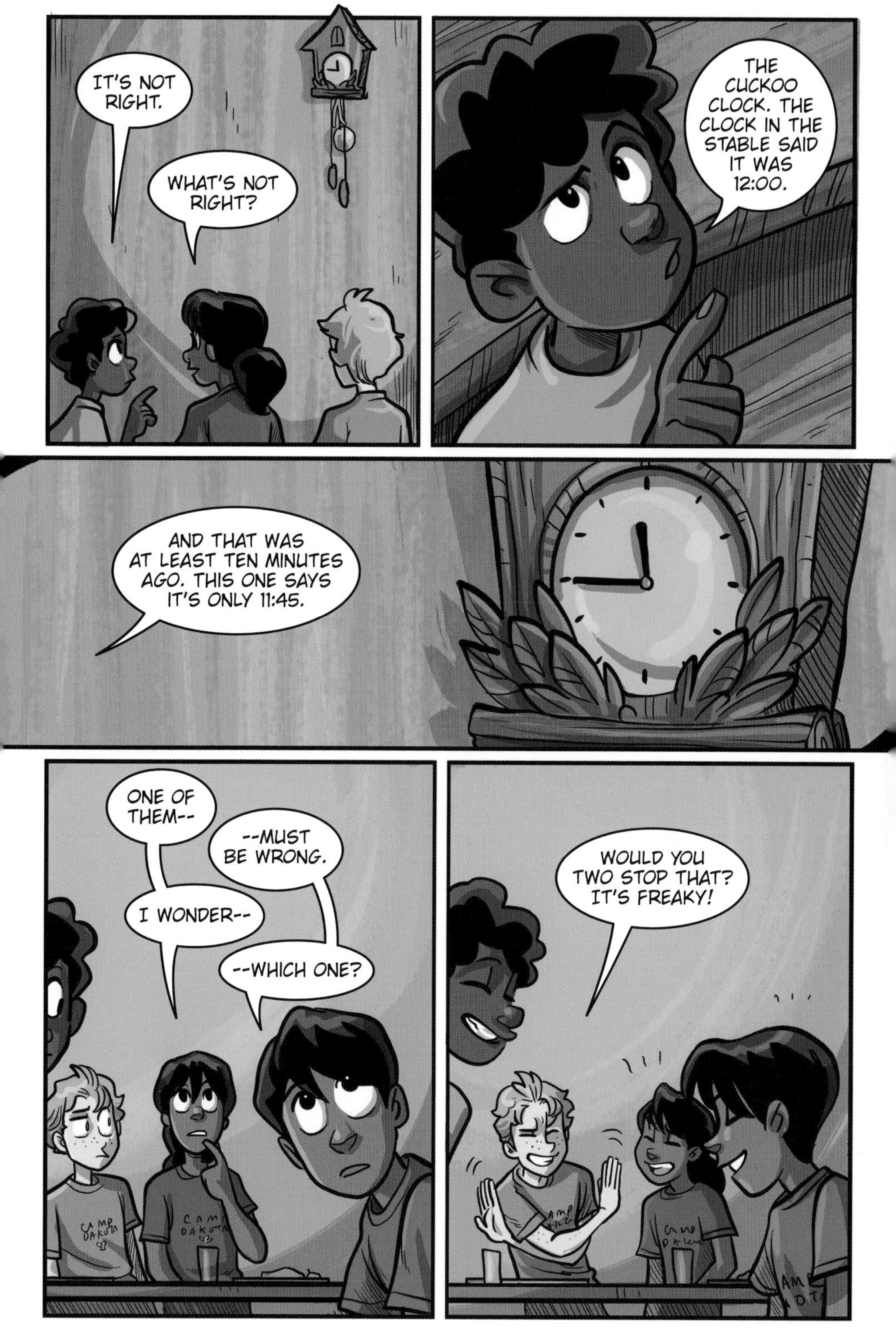

IT'S NOT RIGHT.
WHAT'S NOT RIGHT?
THE CUCKOO CLOCK. THE CLOCK IN THE STABLE SAID IT WAS 12:00.
AND THAT WAS AT LEAST TEN MINUTES AGO. THIS ONE SAYS IT'S ONLY 11:45.
ONE OF THEM--
--MUST BE WRONG.
I WONDER--
--WHICH ONE?
WOULD YOU TWO STOP THAT? IT'S FREAKY!

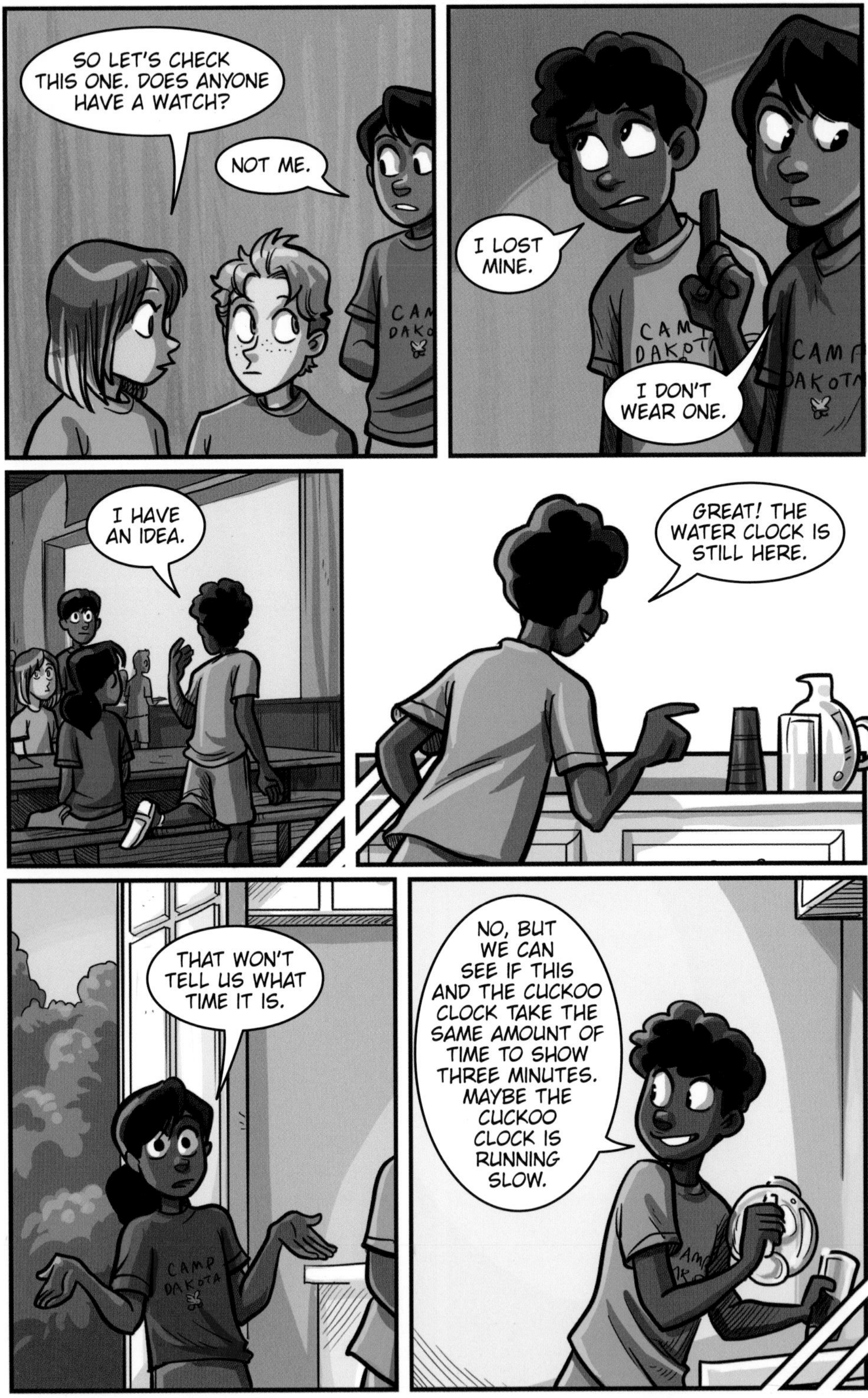
SO LET'S CHECK THIS ONE. DOES ANYONE HAVE A WATCH?
NOT ME.
I LOST MINE.
I DON'T WEAR ONE.
I HAVE AN IDEA.
GREAT! THE WATER CLOCK IS STILL HERE.
THAT WON'T TELL US WHAT TIME IT IS.
NO, BUT WE CAN SEE IF THIS AND THE CUCKOO CLOCK TAKE THE SAME AMOUNT OF TIME TO SHOW THREE MINUTES. MAYBE THE CUCKOO CLOCK IS RUNNING SLOW.
CAMP DAKOTA

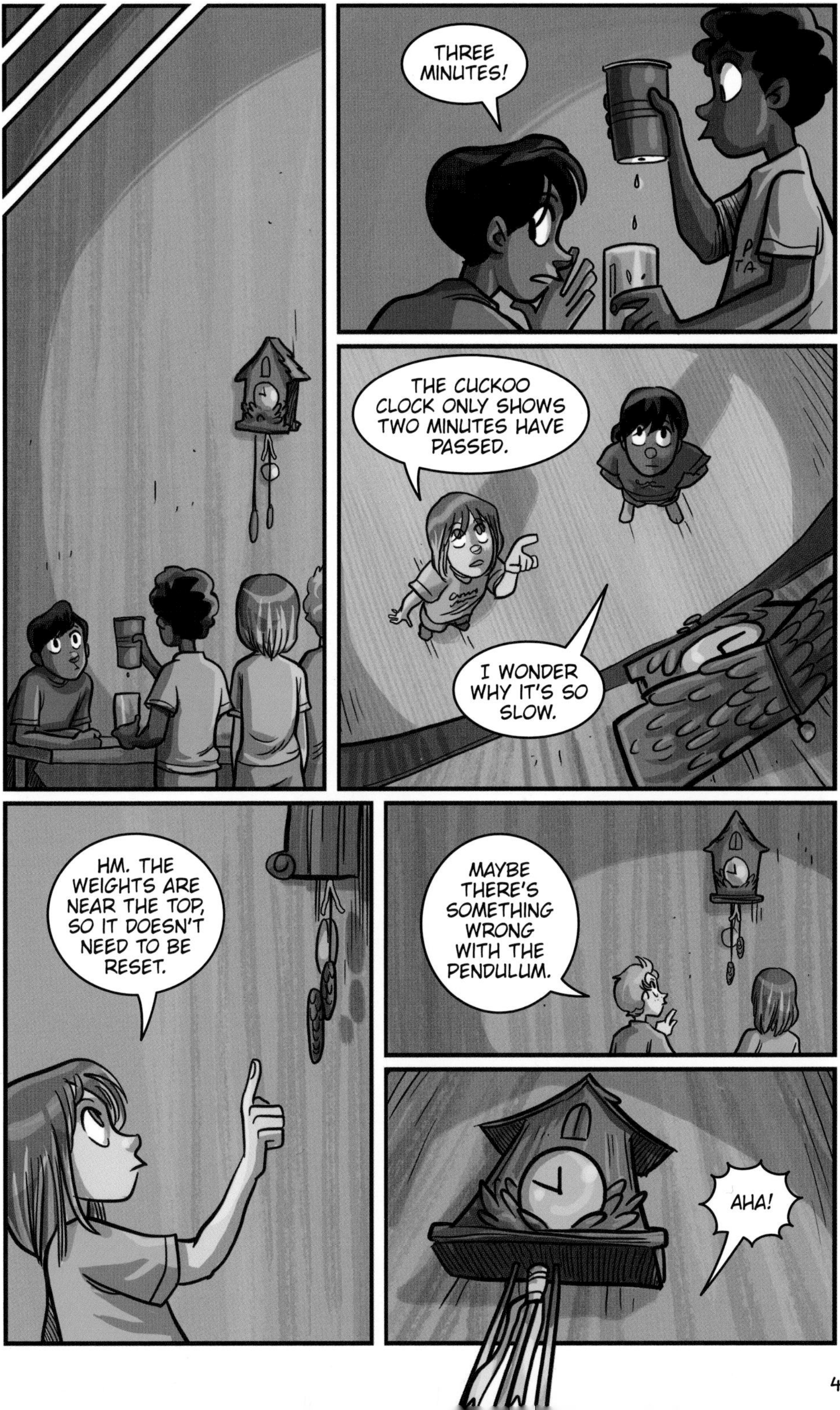
THREE MINUTES!
THE CUCKOO CLOCK ONLY SHOWS TWO MINUTES HAVE PASSED.
I WONDER WHY IT'S SO SLOW.
HM. THE WEIGHTS ARE NEAR THE TOP, SO IT DOESN'T NEED TO BE RESET.
MAYBE THERE'S SOMETHING WRONG WITH THE PENDULUM.
AHA!

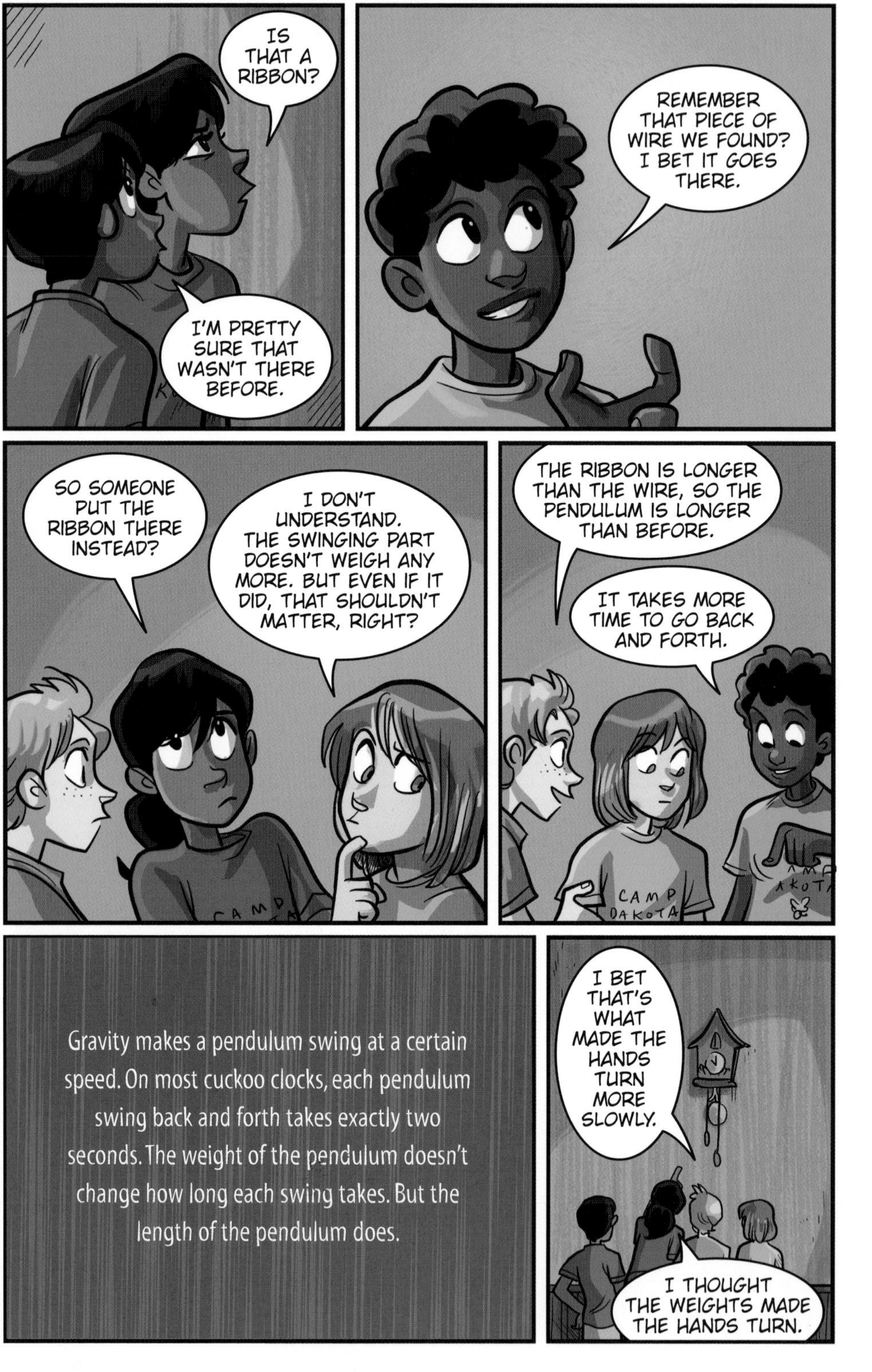
IS THAT A RIBBON?
I'M PRETTY SURE THAT WASN'T THERE BEFORE.
REMEMBER THAT PIECE OF WIRE WE FOUND? I BET IT GOES THERE.
SO SOMEONE PUT THE RIBBON THERE INSTEAD?
I DON'T UNDERSTAND. THE SWINGING PART DOESN'T WEIGH ANY MORE. BUT EVEN IF IT DID, THAT SHOULDN'T MATTER, RIGHT?
THE RIBBON IS LONGER THAN THE WIRE, SO THE PENDULUM IS LONGER THAN BEFORE.
IT TAKES MORE TIME TO GO BACK AND FORTH.
Gravity makes a pendulum swing at a certain speed. On most cuckoo clocks, each pendulum swing back and forth takes exactly two seconds. The weight of the pendulum doesn't change how long each swing takes. But the length of the pendulum does.
I BET THAT'S WHAT MADE THE HANDS TURN MORE SLOWLY.
I THOUGHT THE WEIGHTS MADE THE HANDS TURN.

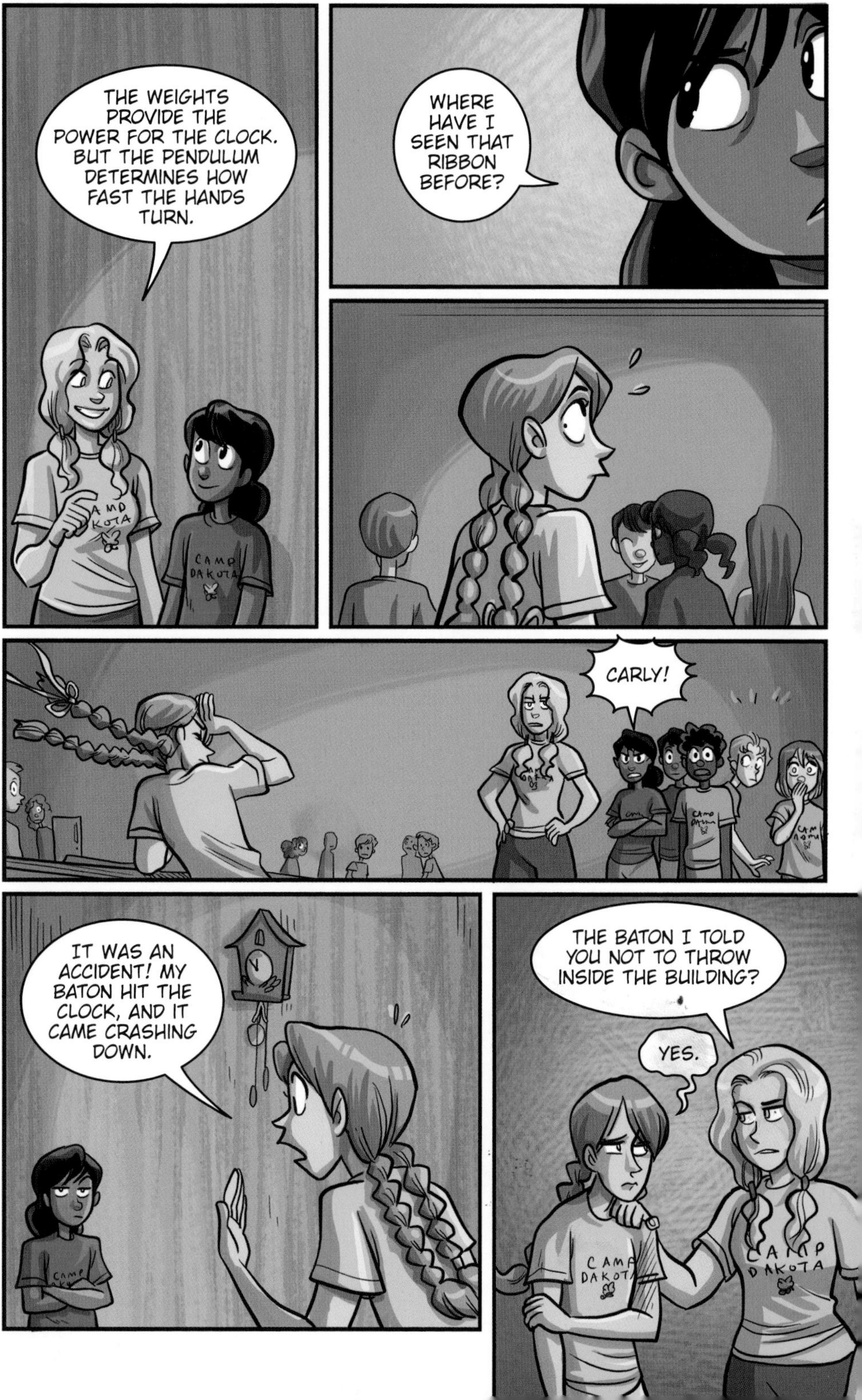
THE WEIGHTS PROVIDE THE POWER FOR THE CLOCK. BUT THE PENDULUM DETERMINES HOW FAST THE HANDS TURN.
WHERE HAVE I SEEN THAT RIBBON BEFORE?
CARLY!
IT WAS AN ACCIDENT! MY BATON HIT THE CLOCK, AND IT CAME CRASHING DOWN.
THE BATON I TOLD YOU NOT TO THROW INSIDE THE BUILDING?
YES.

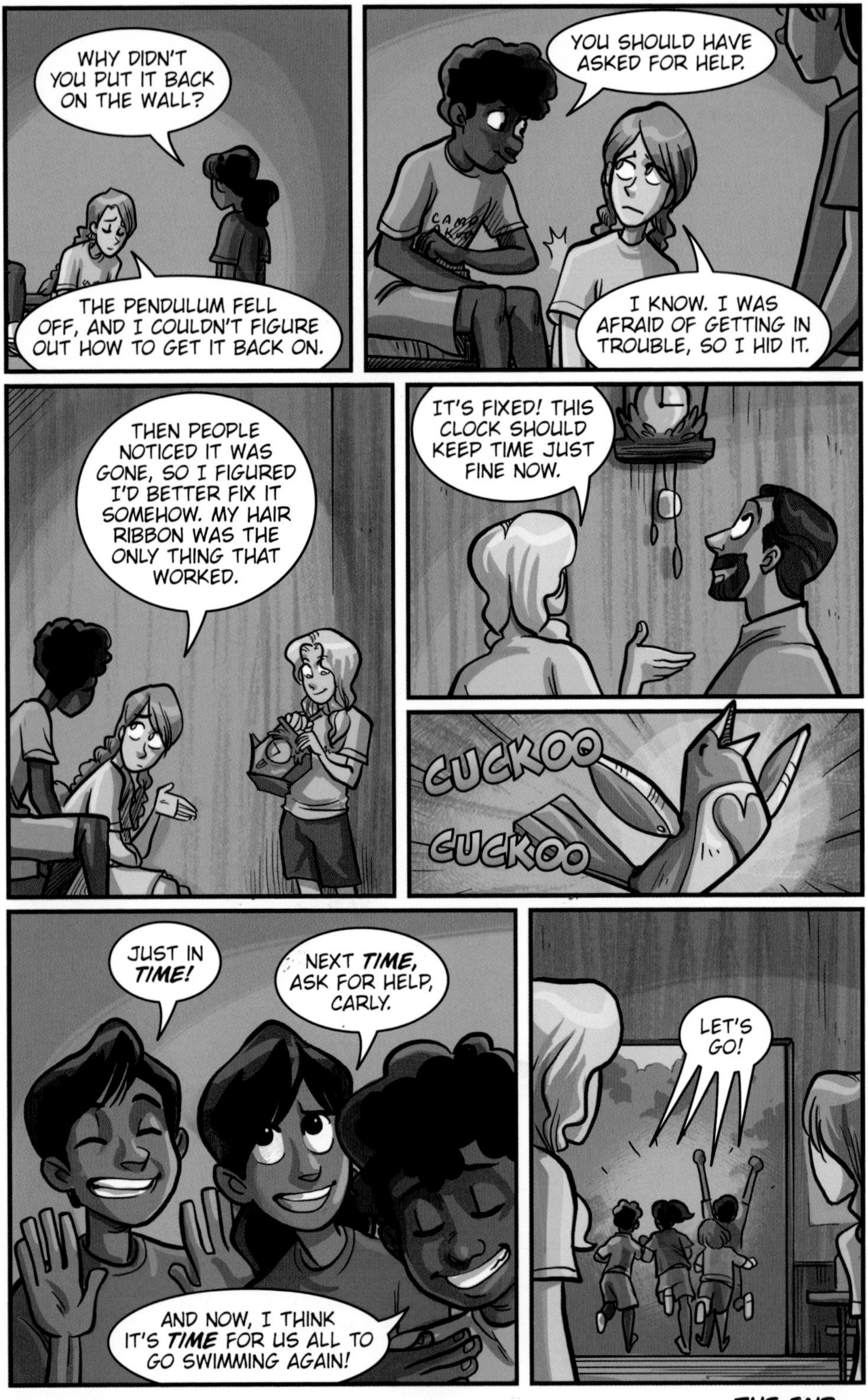
WHY DIDN'T YOU PUT IT BACK ON THE WALL?
THE PENDULUM FELL OFF, AND I COULDN'T FIGURE OUT HOW TO GET IT BACK ON.
YOU SHOULD HAVE ASKED FOR HELP.
I KNOW. I WAS AFRAID OF GETTING IN TROUBLE, SO I HID IT.
THEN PEOPLE NOTICED IT WAS GONE, SO I FIGURED I'D BETTER FIX IT SOMEHOW. MY HAIR RIBBON WAS THE ONLY THING THAT WORKED.
IT'S FIXED! THIS CLOCK SHOULD KEEP TIME JUST FINE NOW.
CUCKOO
CUCKOO
JUST IN *TIME!*
NEXT *TIME,* ASK FOR HELP, CARLY.
AND NOW, I THINK IT'S *TIME* FOR US ALL TO GO SWIMMING AGAIN!
LET'S GO!

THE END

Experiments

Try these fun experiments at home or in your classroom.
Make sure you have an adult help out.

Uphill Battle

You will need: jar lid, 3 marbles, 2 rubber bands, tape, piece of cardboard

1)   Put two rubber bands around the outside of the jar lid.
2)   On the inside of the jar lid, tape three marbles, side by side, just inside the outer edge.
3)   Make a fold near one edge of the cardboard to form a ramp.
4)   Hold the jar lid on its edge at the bottom of the ramp. Make sure the marbles are almost at the top of the lid, on the side going up the ramp.
5)   Let go of the jar lid and watch it roll up the ramp instead of down.

What Happened?

Gravity pulls on the heaviest part of an object. The marbles made one side of the lid heavier than the other. Gravity pulled them down, making the lid roll up!

Make Your Own Pendulum

You will need: hex nuts, string, tape, stopwatch or watch with a second hand

First, experiment with pendulums that have different weights.

1) Tape one end of the string to a desk or table so the string hangs down and can swing freely.
2) Cut the string to a length where it doesn't touch the ground.
3) Tie a hex nut to the free end of the string.
4) Pull the hex nut up to the level of the table with the string held taut.
5) Let go of the hex nut, and time how long it takes for the nut to swing forward and back.
6) Now tie a second hex nut to the end of the string. Swing and time it again.

Was there a difference in the times?

Now try changing the length of your pendulum.

1) Cut some length off the bottom of your string, making it shorter.
2) Attach a hex nut to the free end.
3) Time the length of the pendulum swing as you did before.

How did this time compare to the time from the longer string?

What Happened?

Adding weight didn't change the time of the pendulum swing, because gravity pulls the same on all objects dropped from the same height, regardless of their weight.

The shorter length of string did change the time of the swing. The length of the pendulum is what determines the time it takes to swing.

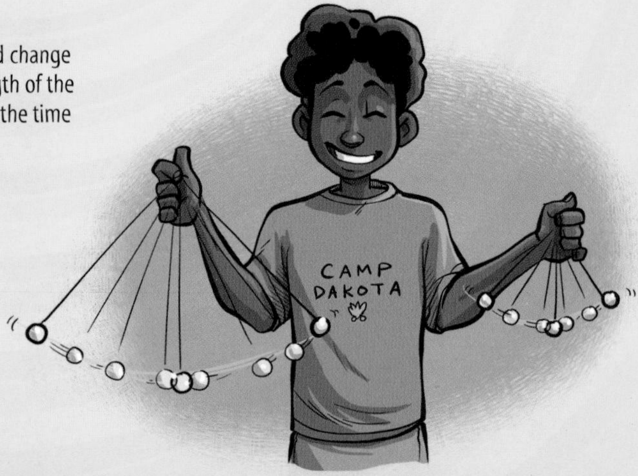
CAMP
DAKOTA